THE
CENTER
OF THE
UNIVERSE

→ Yep, that would be ME

ALSO BY **ANITA LIBERTY**

How to Heal the Hurt by Hating

How to Stay Bitter
Through the Happiest Times of Your Life

THE CENTER OF THE UNIVERSE

yep, that would be

ME

This is a book about being a teenager.
Being a teenager <u>sucks</u>!
Enjoy the book.

ANITA LIBERTY

SIMON PULSE   New York   London   Toronto   Sydney

SIMON PULSE · An imprint of Simon & Schuster Children's Publishing Division · 1230 Avenue of the Americas, New York, NY 10020 · Copyright © 2008 by Suzanne Weber · All rights reserved, including the right of reproduction in whole or in part in any form. · SIMON PULSE and colophon are registered trademarks of Simon & Schuster, Inc. · Designed by Jessica Sonkin · The text of this book was set in Fairfield Light. · Manufactured in the United States of America · First Simon Pulse edition July 2008 · 10 9 8 7 6 5 4 3 2 1 · Library of Congress Control Number 2007940383 · ISBN-13: 978-1-4169-5789-8 · ISBN-10: 1-4169-5789-8

For my parents.

I forgive you.

THE
CENTER
OF THE
UNIVERSE

yep, that would be ME

THE CENTER OF THE UNIVERSE
by Anita Liberty, age 13

That would be me.

The Center of the Universe.

No one here but me.

And They say the world doesn't revolve around Anita Liberty!

HA!

HA!

I'll show them.

They just don't understand the burden

of my position.

It carries a lot of weight.

And I wait . . .

and wait . . .

and wait . . .

for the lifeblood of my womanhood

to begin coursing through the cavity of

my ever-changing body.

And until it does, I am caught in the purgatory that is puberty.

And They act as if everything's completely normal.

They ask me, "How was the math test?"

As if I care about the math test.

They ask me, "How's school?"

as if that question doesn't send a burning spear

through the soft palate of my adolescence.

They ask me "What's new?"

As if I could explain the constantly evolving reality

of my own desperate existence.

They ask me, "Why are you so irritable all the time?"

As if I could suppress the persistent anger

that feeds off of the convention of our nuclear family.

They don't understand that I was put here

for a **higher purpose**.

Don't ask me any questions . . .

about **anything**.

Don't expect me to be polite . . .

to **anyone**.

Don't look at me . . .

not even a **glance in my direction**.

Or I just might lose it.

Parents suck.

PREFACE
by Anita Liberty
(the full-grown, very mature, non-teenage,
adult one, that is)

I wrote that poem, "The Center of the Universe," a long time ago. I included it in my first book, *How to Heal the Hurt by Hating*, because I felt that it was relevant to see how the bitter woman was first a bitter teenager—like anyone needed proof. I'm including it here and, in fact, beginning this book with it because, well, I needed it to fulfill the page count I promised my editor. But I also believe it helps to set the tone of this book, the one you hold in your lucky little hands right now. Even though this book will cover my life from the ages of sixteen through eighteen, I think that the poem "The Center of the Universe" is an accurate representation of how I felt during all seven of the years that I was a teenager. Actually, it's a pretty accurate representation of how I feel right now— many, many years beyond my teenage ones. I still feel like I'm the center of the universe, and I still don't feel that anyone is acknowledging that I was put here for a higher purpose.

I had the idea for writing this book when I recently unearthed a box of journals and notebooks and schoolwork from my high school years. My mother called me and asked me to come over to my parents' home and clear out some of the boxes I'd left there when I went to college. She said she needed the space. She said that I'd been promising to move them for the last seventeen years. She said she wasn't going to ask me again. I told her that it would be no problem and that I was really, really sorry that I hadn't done it before, but I was glad to come over and remove them because I didn't want her to be inconvenienced in any way by my negligence. And then I told her how much I loved her and what a fantastic mother she was and how she was really more like a friend than a mother. Because, y'know all that anger and annoyance you feel at your parents when you're a teenager? It just goes away as soon as you hit your twenties. You forgive them their faults, you start appreciating their strengths, you listen to their advice and give them the respect that they're due.

Right. That is exactly *not* what happens. At all. I told my mother that I was extremely busy right now and that I would get to it when I had time and did she need me to go to the hardware store to buy her a flashlight so she could see which direction she needed to go in order to crawl out of my ass? See? It never ends.

Anyway, I did finally give in and go to my parents' place to sort through some of the boxes. And I uncovered *treasure*. I found several journals, scads of poetry, my yearbook from my senior year, and my old SAT workbook. I spent hours going through the "material" ('cause, really, everything I've ever written or experienced or thought about ends up becoming material for my art), and it was informative and painful and reassuring all at the same time. Sort of like the whole experience of high school. And life. And reading my books. As you're about to find out.

4

~~My name is Anita Li.~~ That was stupid. Why am I introducing myself? It's like I'm writing this for some stranger who might be reading this. I don't want a stranger reading this. It's my private diary. PRIVATE. Unless of course, maybe someday, waaaay in the future, I become famous (for what? who cares?) and this journal will be published. But by then my name will be on the cover of the book and everyone will already know who I am and so I won't need to introduce myself. I will, however, need to give a bit of *context* for these mythical future readers.

I'm sixteen.

I'm going to be a junior in high school.

I'm single—meaning that I don't have a boyfriend, not that I'm not married. But I'm not. Married. And anyway, how could I be married when I haven't even ever had a boy-friend? I mean, to be married would mean that SOMEONE WOULD HAVE HAD TO FIND ME ATTRACTIVE FOR AT LEAST LIKE A FUCKING MINUTE! And that hasn't happened yet. At least not to my face. I'm sure there are all kinds of crushes on me happening behind my back and the cutest boys in school are all too shy and intimidated by me to approach me. That's probably what's going on.

What else?

I have parents. I'm mad at them right now. Well, that's not news. That would be true at almost any given moment. They treat me like they have no idea who I am, like I just walked into their home and started making myself a peanut butter sandwich. My very presence seems to confuse and irritate them. Like, for instance, I got my hair cut the other day and it wasn't a good cut. It just wasn't. And I told my mom that I was dissatisfied with it, and she asked if I wanted to go back and get it fixed, and I was like, "But it's already too short!" And then she started yelling at me, saying, "Well, what do you want me to do? You're being unreasonable. Blah, blah, blah!" Whatever. I don't care how mean they are to me. I have a secret plan. . . . If my parents don't shape up and start being nice to me soon, I'll just refuse to take care of them when they're old. And isn't that pretty much why people have kids to begin with? So they have someone who'll take care of them when they're decrepit and senile and weak? I'm keeping track. I'm going to buy a ledger and document each and every one of their infractions. It's all gonna add up. I guess they'll just have to rely on my sister.

I have a sister. A younger sister. Her name is Hope (awww, how cute . . . blech) and she's four years my junior. She's just about to hit puberty. And I think she's gonna hit it hard. She's already annoying as hell, and I don't see that letting up anytime soon. I think she's going to be acting premenstrual until she actually menstruates. However, for some reason she's already managed to get herself a boyfriend. I don't think they actually *do* anything, but it is a blow to my ego that my twelve-year-old sister is in a committed relationship with a guy and I'm not. In a committed relationship with a guy. Or in any kind of relationship with a guy, if we're to get technical.

My best friends are Victoria, Alexandra, and Jessica.

Victoria is really cool. She's an amazing artist. And a lot less anxious than I am. She keeps me grounded. Well, as grounded as I can be, which is still about twelve feet off the ground. And she understands me, and that's pretty much all I care about—being understood.

Alexandra and I have been friends since first grade. Well, we've known each other since first grade. We have one of those hot-and-cold relationships. She can be pretty oblivious to other people's feelings, and I sometimes get annoyed at her superficiality. But we're also really close. She has a lot of experience with boys. She was an au pair this summer in the Hamptons for this really rich family and she met this guy and they went skinny-dipping every morning before her family woke up. I mean, come on! That's so sexy. That's like a complete fantasy. Alexandra has a high status at school, so sometimes it's fun hanging around her because then I feel like I have a high status just by association. Other times I feel like her high status just highlights my stumpy status.

She calls the shots in our relationship. And I hate myself for letting her.

Jessica is a relatively new friend of mine. She just transferred to our school in ninth grade. She moved to New York from down South, so she has this really cute accent. I like her. She's got big boobs. I mean, that's not *why* I like her—duh—but I'm just sayin', it's one of her defining characteristics. From a completely objective viewpoint. Also, she has a really cute older brother who's in college, so he's completely unattainable, but it's way fun to be over there when he's home on a break from school 'cause he's freakin' hot.

I write poetry.

I need some new clothes.

I need some new friends.

I need a boyfriend.

I need a new attitude (if you ask my parents, but don't . . .).

HIGH SCHOOL

In the future,
when I am an adult,
I will imagine myself reliving high school.
But this time
I'm the cool girl.
And I **hate** all my friends.
They are so bossy,
always trying to get me to do what they want
when I only care about what I want.
I don't succumb to peer pressure.
I smoke because I want to
and it makes me look ultracool
(and it doesn't make me want to throw up).
I listen to loud music
and stay out late.
And I'm looking for a **bad** boy
to piss off my parents.
He has to be beautiful
and **sullen**
and confused
so that I can come into his life
and save him.
If you know him, call him
and tell him the cool girl is looking for him.

She wants to make out.

ADVICE FROM ANITA LIBERTY

When you write a poem about your MOST INTIMATE
YEARNINGS, remember not to carry it around with
you and then get distracted by the idea of making
nachos for yourself and then eat those nachos (note:
quality of salsa = quality of nachos) and then go watch
television and fall asleep in a melted-cheese-induced
stupor and wake up to see your parents standing
there staring at you and realize that they're holding
the poem about your MOST INTIMATE YEARNINGS
because you left it on the kitchen counter. If this
happens, you're going to have to endure a lecture
about the evils of smoking (like I don't know) and about
how being cool isn't really all that important, and now
you have to denounce your own poem about your MOST
INTIMATE YEARNINGS as a joke. And that will hurt.

PARENTAL INFRACTION (Brief Description)	LEVEL OF ANNOYANCE 1-10 scale: 1 being Easily Forgivable, 10 being Committed to a Nursing Home the Minute They Hit 70
Reading something that was not meant for them to see in the first place and then lecturing me about the content	6

School starts in a week. My junior year. Three hundred and twenty school days until graduation from high school. Not that I'm counting. I haven't figured out what I'm wearing for the first day of school. I guess knowing where all my clothes are would help. Why don't I know where all my clothes are? BECAUSE I HAVE NO IDEA WHERE ANYTHING IS, thanks to the fact that we moved a couple weeks ago. Where was I when my parents were hatching this brilliant scheme to move us into Manhattan from Brooklyn? Into a desolate part of the city where I can't go out alone late at night? Where I have to take the subway in to school every morning? Thank God I don't have to change schools. Oh man, I would have had to literally kill my parents if that was the case. I've been at the same school since first grade. It's a private school and I've been looking forward to being a junior for as long as I can remember so that I could come home for free periods and come home for lunch, etc. Now I'm too far away to do that, so I'll be stuck wandering the streets eating a piece of pizza during lunch instead of coming home and watching television and making nachos. Stupid, stupid, stupid. Am I not part of this family? Am I not to be consulted on major life decisions that affect my life majorly? I loved our old house. I loved living near all my friends. I loved my room, my walk-in closet where I could hide, where I'd been hiding since I was five, the street we lived on. Here at our new "loft" I don't have a room. I don't even have a freaking door! My parents took the one room that is an actual room. They gave my sister a bed in a hallway in the back (not so great for her, either, but that's her problem—she's got to learn how to fight her own fights). And I have a platform in the MIDDLE of the whole space. A platform!! It's like I'm on a fucking *stage*. No, I'm sorry, it's not *like* I'm on a fucking stage. I *am* on a fucking stage. I've figured out that there are just two places where I can stand and no one can see me. One is over by the closet with the door open, and the other is crouching down behind my bed. I'm going to install red velvet curtains that I can close when the fucking show of my life is over. My parents told me they thought that sleeping on a platform in the middle of the loft would be "fun" for me. My parents have no fucking clue what would be "fun" for me. They wouldn't know "fun" if it ran up and pinched their nipples.

So here I am. Stuck on my platform stage. Living my teenage life for everyone to see. On second thought maybe I can make this work for me.

I can set up a microphone.

And do a one-person show.

And serve drinks.

And charge admission.

And sell T-shirts—T-shirts that say:

I'M HAVING A CRISIS. WANNA WATCH?

and

MY PARENTS ARE ASS-CLOWNS.

and

FUCK OFF.

Order yours now.

PARENTAL INFRACTION (Brief Description)	LEVEL OF ANNOYANCE 1-10 scale: 1 being Easily Forgivable, 10 being Committed to a Nursing Home the Minute They Hit 70
Reading something that was not meant for them to see in the first place and then lecturing me about the content	6
Moving our family to an unrenovated undivided loft space and then putting me on a PLATFORM in the middle of it	10

THE LITTLE VISITOR

I see you and
I want to kill you—
make you die
like the vermin
you are.
Crush you under my shoe.
Smash your little skull.
But...
you are so cute.

Confident in knowing
you can find that place in me,
you stroll to the middle of
my ~~bedroom~~ platform,
look right at me,
and clean your
little, tiny whiskers.

You dance around the carefully laid glue traps.
You skillfully avoid the snap traps.
You show uncharacteristic restraint
by refusing to eat the poison the exterminator
promised would put an end to you and your family.

I can hear you.
I know you're there.

And I will not rest until you die.

You are very,

VERY

cute,

and I hate you.

We have a mouse. And it appears to have set up its little mouse house in the closet of what I would call my bedroom if it were actually a **ROOM**. I hear it in the middle of the night. It freaks me out, but I'm conflicted. My parents won't let me and Hope have any pets, so this is the closest I think I'll get. That's not true. They did get me a hamster when I was about ten, but it was a vicious little creature. Alexandra had a hamster named Marshmallow, who would curl up in the crook of her legs and fall asleep while she pet it. It was the sweetest thing. I begged my parents to let me have one. They finally relented (a rarity for them—so stubborn are they) and bought me a hamster that I named Tamale. That might have been part of the problem, actually. Alexandra's hamster, Marshmallow, was sweet and soft and benign. My hamster, Tamale, was hot-tempered and fiery and made me want to cry. I remember that whenever it was time to clean his cage, my dad would go into my room wearing huge, thick rubber gloves and protective goggles. (What? Like Tamale was going to launch himself at my dad's eyeball? Maybe, actually.) He would lift Tamale out of his cage and I would put in the fresh newspaper. Whenever I tried to interact with Tamale, he would stand on his hind legs and hold the bars of his cage in his tiny hamster fists and shake the bars like he was a prison inmate trying to get my attention so he could plead the case for his innocence. And then I woke up one morning and the whole side of Tamale's face (do hamsters have faces?) was swollen up. I thought he had something in his cheek, but he didn't, and his eye was swollen shut and it was all goopy. It didn't look good. We called the vet and he told us that it was some kind of infection and that we should bring him in so that he could put him to sleep. I cried a lot. I mean, I didn't really even like the stupid animal, but I didn't like the idea of paying someone to kill him. I would have cuddled him and kissed him good-bye, but I didn't want to lose a lip, so I just sort of waved at him while my dad put him in a cardboard box and took him off to the vet to meet his ultimate fate. My tears dried pretty quickly and I had already moved on by the time my dad returned home an hour later with the cardboard box in hand. I really didn't want to see Tamale's still little body, so I thought it was kind of morbid that Dad had brought it home, but my dad was smiling. He seemed really pleased with himself. He opened the box and there was Tamale. Alive. My dad then produced a medicine bottle and an eye dropper and explained that the vet had given him antibiotics for the beastlet. I can't say I was pleased. I'd already mourned the loss of Tamale, and even that had ended up taking more energy than it was worth, given how little he contributed to my life in terms of warmth and affection. My dad dutifully suited up every night and administered the medication to Tamale. Tamale died two weeks later anyway. Oh well. It wasn't a lot of fun having a hamster. And it's not a lot of fun having a mouse. But it's not totally dissimilar.

However, apparently my father sees no parallel at all between hamsters and mice, since he's insisting on catching the mouse with glue traps, which I find completely inhumane. Then again, so is putting your teenage daughter on a platform in the middle of your apartment, Dad.

20

PARENTAL INFRACTION (Brief Description)	LEVEL OF ANNOYANCE 1-10 scale, 1 being Easily Forgivable, 10 being Committed to a Nursing Home the Minute They Hit 70
Reading something that was not meant for them to see in the first place and then lecturing me about the content	6
Moving our family to a RODENT-INFESTED unrenovated undivided loft space and then putting me on a PLATFORM in the middle of it	10
Saving a rodent I didn't care about from an untimely (or timely) death	3

THE BREAKDOWN

Who will earn my affections this year?
Which boy will be lucky enough to have me?
Who will end up with me as the prize?

There are the **boys** who are completely unattainable,
but they're completely unattainable.
There are the **boys** who are cute, but *just* cute.
There are the **boys** who are nice, but *just* nice.
There are the **boys** who are so cool that they make me
feel like a loser.
There are the **boys** who are such losers that they make me
feel like a loser.
There are the **boys** I've known since second grade who still
act like they're in second grade.
There are the **boys** I don't like . . .
and that's not gonna change.

And I'd say that's pretty much it.
I guess I'll be spending another year alone.

Big surprise.

An SAT Word from <u>Anita Liberty</u>

in·cho·ate

(adj.) unformed or formless; in a beginning stage

Anita Liberty's feelings about the boys in her grade were <u>inchoate</u> prior to the start of school, since she hadn't yet had a chance to see who had gotten cuter over the summer and who had gotten dorkier.

School started today. I was pleasantly surprised, because all the boys looked pretty cute to me. Even the ones who usually aren't. But I guess it was sort of like going to a supermarket when you're starving—you end up buying a bunch of crap and finding out that you bought nothing you can actually eat for dinner. Although sometimes plowing through a box of Oreos and skipping dinner altogether can be fun. Seriously, though, I'm smack-dab in the middle of my high school years and I need to find a boyfriend. Now. Danny B. looked adorable, but he's so weird. Mark L. was also really flirty with me, but he's just not cool enough. Tommy B. was looking seriously cute. He seems older than the other boys in my grade. I wonder if that's because he's so tall. God, I wish he weren't so damned tall. Or that I wasn't so damned short. I'm so short. Why am I so freaking short? I don't feel like I'm supposed to be this short. But I guess, now that I'm sixteen, that I'm done growing. This is how tall (or how short) I'm gonna be: five feet two inches. That sounds reasonable, but most of my friends are way taller. I feel like my height makes my friends infantilize me. They make me sit on their laps. They reach for my hand when we cross the street. It's humiliating. And, since I'm so tiny, the amount of humiliation I have to suffer per square inch of me is way more intense than some of my taller and better-built friends.

But, hey, it's a new year. And I'm trying (desperately) to start this year off with a new attitude. I have only 319 more school days until graduation, and I'm going to turn over a new leaf. I'm going to try not to be so negative. I'm going to let things roll off my back. I'm going to try to be *cheerful* and see where that lands me.

MY STATE OF BEING

Forged from the depths of my misery,
I sprang from my own head.
Unlocked my own box.
Gave birth to myself.
(It wasn't pretty.)

Every feeling I've ever had
gets noted and catalogued.
Documented for those who want to **know**.
And I believe everyone wants to **know**.
Who wouldn't want to **know**?
Know what it's like to get sucked
into the whirlpool of despair
and be spit out on the other side—
digested and consumed by my own fear of rejection.

I'm no different from you.
No different.
I am you.
What you keep inside and keep from spilling out,
I unapologetically scream from the rooftops.
I am the one who sacrifices herself
so that you can be purged.
No one's different.
We're all the same.
Just in different stages of emotional evolution.

In other words,

while you still squirm around in the primordial **o o z e** ,

I stand

ERECT.

An SAT Word from _Anita Liberty_

sa·gac·i·ty
(n.) shrewdness; soundness of perspective

With remarkable _sagacity_ Anita Liberty's poem conveyed the inner workings of her adolescent mind. Damn, she's good.

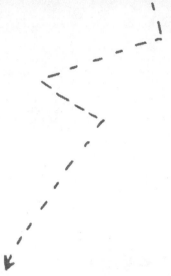

Right. Being cheerful lasted about fourteen minutes. Although, it's only the beginning of October and things might be looking up. Or at least I am. Literally.

Tommy B. and I hung out a lot today. We kept running into each other between classes and flirting. The only issue is that there's like a foot difference in our heights and (sorry for going here) how's that gonna work when we start dating and kissing and . . . having sex? I guess I should take it one step at a time. I've just recently realized that I have a crush on him, and I already have us in bed having awkward, mismatched sex. I will say that my neck does kind of hurt from looking up at him so much. Anyway, we were hanging out at lunch today (we were sitting down against a wall, which is the only way we can kind of see eye to eye) and we were goofing around and kind of pushing each other back and forth. At one point he grabbed my foot and looked at it and then looked at me kind of funny. I then realized that I had written "I adore T.B." on the bottom of my sneaker.

29

ADVICE FROM ANITA LIBERTY

Don't write anything on your shoe that you don't want people to see.

Ya moron.

Today Tommy B. and I were sitting against the lockers on the ninth floor and he jokingly tried to look down my shirt and I jokingly acted like I was offended. I'd say things are progressing nicely.

He's really sweet, although a bit odd. He just seems awkward. Again, maybe it's due to the difference in our heights. I like flirting with him and I like the *idea* of having a boyfriend. And here's where I get confused. Do I really like Tommy B.? Or do I just like the idea of having a boyfriend? In other words, which came first . . . the attraction for the boy or the desire for a boyfriend? It's just that the whole notion of me having a boyfriend is so random and elusive. . . . I might as well fantasize about walking down the street and being stopped by a photographer from *Seventeen* magazine who tells me that he's never seen someone who has such a fresh and natural beauty, and even though I'm about nine inches too short to be an actual model, he's interested in photographing me for a spread in their magazine featuring beautiful, normal *short* girls and that I'll get to keep all the clothes they buy for the shoot. Oh, and would I mind flying first-class to Paris because that's where they've scouted the location and I'd have to stay for a month and get paid a buttload of money—how does that sound? Not that I've actually ever *had* that fantasy.

I wish I could find
the guy who holds
the key
to my heart.
Or maybe it's that
I'm supposed to
change the lock
on my heart
to fit his key?
That sounds like a
lot of work.

THE PHONE CALL
(A Verbatim Transcript)

Ring Ring (That's the phone.)

Anita: (picking up phone): Hello?

Male voice: Hey.

Anita: Hey.

Male voice: What's up?

Anita: Tommy?

Tommy: Yeah. Oh, yeah. Sorry. It's Tommy.

Anita: Umm . . . hey. What's up?

Tommy: Nothing much. What's up with you?

Anita: Nothing.

Silence.

Tommy: Cool.

Anita: Cool.

Tommy: Just thought I'd call and say "hey."

Anita: Hey.

Tommy: And, maybe, uh, y'know, would you like to see a movie sometime?

Anita: Oh. Okay. Yeah. Sure.

Tommy: Great. Okay. See ya in school tomorrow.

Anita: Okay.

Tommy: Take it easy.

Anita: I will.

Tommy: But take it.

Anita: What?

Tommy: But take it.

Anita: Okay. What?

Tommy: Take it easy. But take it.

Anita: Oh. Okay. I will. So long.

Tommy: Yeah. Bye.

Anita: Bye.

An SAT Word from _Anita Liberty_

tran·si·to·ry

(adj.) not permanent or lasting but existing only for a short time

Anita realized, after a very dull and somewhat annoying phone call from Tommy B., that her feelings for him were transitory.

I'm totally not interested in Tommy B. anymore. I think mostly 'cause he started liking me back. And, if that's my pattern, that's gonna be a problem in terms of me finding a boyfriend. Unless, of course, I just continually attempt to date people who don't like me. Which is a distinct possibility.

However, the big news is that our school is doing an exchange program with some school in France, and the French kids arrived today. They're staying for two weeks. The idea behind this kind of exchange program is that the students come here to attend classes, have homestays, improve their English, and just generally experience life in America. Uh-huh. Whatever. All I know is that these boys are here to give me a reason to get up in the morning. Christ, they are glorious. I'd do any of them. Or all of them. At one time. In the girls' bathroom. After school. Between classes. *During* class.

The leader of the *brûlant* pack is Jean-François. He is a true French fox (I guess that would make him a *renard*). And guess who pounced on him right away and started making out with him tonight at Alexandra's party? Alexandra? *Non.* Jessica? *Non.* Victoria? *Non.* Moi? *Oui! Non! Oui! Non!! OUI! OUI! OUI! Moi, moi, moi.* It was delicious. Amazing. J-F is an incredible kisser. Oh, but he made out so well. He gave me a hicky! My first real one. He did these incredible things with his tongue on my neck. It made me shiver. And it seemed like he was really just into making out. He didn't try to unbutton my pants or even feel me up. *Je suis une idole sexuelle.* Maybe I'll lose my virginity to a sexy French boy, and then, once he goes back to France, we'll write letters back and forth proclaiming our devotion to each other and our desire for each other and I'll move to Paris after I graduate. My parents will freak, and that will make it even more fun.

On another note, I've been hanging out a lot with this girl Sherry. She's cool. I never really paid much attention to her before, but she's as much into the French guys as I am, so I guess we've found our common ground. It's nice to have a new friend.

I saw Jean-François this morning and he was pretty cold to me. By the afternoon he wasn't even talking to me or acknowledging my presence. Jeez. It wasn't like I was running up to him and throwing my arms around him or expecting an engagement ring or anything. We just made out. Well, so much for Jean-François. I've moved on. (And, oddly, I've been able to. I guess I'm attractive to French boys. I'm on a plane to Paris the minute I'm out from under my parents' roof.) Laurent is equally *formidable*, albeit a little shorter, which is fine with me. At least we can see eye to eye. I mean, he is taller than I am. He's not a midget. And he's incredibly gorgeous. I was thinking about how I could possibly say no if he asked me to sleep with him. It'd be hard. (It'd have to be. Heh-heh.) Doesn't matter since he'll never ask. He seems pretty tentative with me physically. It's fun speaking French all the time. French boys adore American girls. They think we're all easy lays.

39

So Alexandra was fucking Thierry in the bedroom last night, and Sherry and I had to go in a couple times to use the bathroom. It was embarrassing. I'm going to ask Sherry tomorrow if she's a virgin or not. I can't tell. Sherry and I are really good friends now. The French kids left for Washington this evening and won't be back until tomorrow night. There's a transit strike, so Sherry and I will have the perfect excuse to stay at Alexandra's place for the next few nights, since Sherry and I both live in Manhattan and Alexandra's in Brooklyn. I can't wait to see what happens tomorrow when Sherry and I meet the bus from Washington. All these guys kiss your hand and both cheeks constantly. Yay! I'm so happy right now!! (What? Who just wrote that?)

40

FRENCH-KISSING

THEY swarm my port.
THEY invade my territory.
Their need for conquest is palpable.
The arrogance of the French is evident.

All the French boys want to do is French.
THEY don't want to know me.
THEY don't want to learn about how we do things here.
THEY're not interested in romance, friendship,
an exchange of ideas.

THEY want to conquer.
THEY want to win.
THEY want to fuck.

All that the French boys want is . . . me.
I am the unknown.
I am the object of their desire.
THEY think I'm just some hot little American girl
who's psyched to make out.

And **THEY** are right.

res·o·lute

(adj.) firm, determined

With a _resolute_ glint in her eye, Anita Liberty sized
up the French exchange students and chose the one with
whom she would have a passionate and thrilling affair, thus
ending her dry spell of, oh, sixteen years.

LAURENT ET MOI TOUJOURS

Today was the worst day of my life. In the morning Laurent was slightly cold to me, so I took a long walk to sort of clear my head. It worked, and I convinced myself he was just in a bad mood. Aren't Frenchmen known for being mercurial? I went back to school and found Victoria. I told her that he had been weird with me, and she suggested that we go find him and see how he was with me now. We went to look for him, and as we rounded the corner, who's walking down the hall toward us? Laurent! Arm in arm with *Sherry*! I can't believe Sherry would do such a shitty thing to me. This is why you don't make new friends. Too much risk involved. Victoria and I just kept walking, and as soon as we were past them, I started crying hysterically. I just couldn't stop. The whole day anytime anyone would look at me, I would cry. Writing about this is making me cry again. I'm crying right now. And I'm looking in the mirror on my desk while I cry. Man, I'm ugly when I cry. Why couldn't I be one of those girls who are more beautiful when they cry? Their cheeks get flushed, their eyelashes moisten into thick black spikes, tears run lazily down their flawless faces. No, I'm an ugly cryer. That's making me cry harder. Now I seriously look like a gargoyle. Maybe that's why Laurent left me for Sherry. Well, that and I heard she gave him a blow job on the back stairs.

An SAT Word from *Anita Liberty*

per·fid·i·ous
(adj.) disloyal

Sherry's a perfidious little bitch.

LAURENT ET MOI JAMAIS PLUS

TAPPED ASH

Our love was as steady
as the ash on your ever-lit Gauloise cigarette.
Never tapped.
Growing longer and longer.

Carelessly,
suddenly,
you moved
and it was gone.

Fallen.
Fallen
  to
    the
      carpet
        below.
Lost forever.

You weren't careful.
Because **you don't care.**
You have a whole pack to burn up.

And you just rub your foot
over the carpet and
there's barely a smudge
left.

No
one
will
ever
know
where
I
have

fallen.

I'm over it. Laurent and Sherry can totally go fuck themselves. And each other. I've actually been having a great time with Alexandra lately. Victoria doesn't trust her. And she is one of those girls who doesn't seem to hold loyalty in high regard, but when you're on the receiving end of her attention, it feels great. I slept over at her house on Tuesday and Wednesday. On Tuesday Jean-François, Thierry, and this guy Bernard came over. Jean-François wanted to fix me up with Bernard. (Even though he rejected me, I guess he feels like I'm good enough for his friend. . . . Nice.) We were sitting together, and Jean-François said to Alexandra, "He likes her and she likes him. They have four more days, and they just sit there." It was extremely embarrassing. Anyway, I guess that Bernard and I are sort of together. I mean, why the fuck not? No harm, no foul. They'll be leaving soon anyway. At this point I'm on my third *garçon* in nine days. That's a new Frenchie every three days. I'm a ho. A happy ho, but a ho nonetheless. My favorite personality and maker-outer was Jean-François, the cutest was Laurent, and Bernard's better than nothing.

I have to say that at least my French has improved a lot. (And by "French" I do mean the type of kissing, not the language.)

An SAT Math Problem from *Anita Liberty*

Fifteen French students arrive in America and are staying for fourteen days. Four of them are female. One of the boys is immediately taken by a girl who's guaranteed to put out (Alexandra, FYI). One of the boys is trying to run through as many girls as he can in fourteen days. One of them is a two-timing prick. One of them is cute enough. They've been here for a week already. How much time would Anita Liberty have to devote to each of the remaining Frenchies (discounting the ones with whom she has already engaged in some light petting) in order to complete her reign of French Exchange Student domination?

    Ⓐ Four hours.
    Ⓑ Twenty minutes.
    Ⓒ Three days.
    Ⓓ As long as it takes to remove my bra.
    Ⓔ None of the above.

(The answer is E, of course. The time will not be equally divided, since the cuter guys are gonna get more time than the less cute guys. That's just basic math.)

52

There was a good-bye party for the Frenchies last night at school. Bernard and I sat on the front stairs and cuddled. It was nice. I got up at one point to go to the bathroom and ran into Laurent. I started to just walk by him without saying hello, but he caught my arm and (sort of) apologized. He then called me a "tease," but in a really friendly you-have-a-small-piece-of-spinach-between-your-teeth kind of way. Like he was trying to help me out. What the fuck? There was never any *opportunity* to go any further than we did. Then he actually came right out and said that he preferred Sherry to me. Maybe he was translating his French thoughts into bad English, but still. He also said that he wanted to see me next year when I'm a woman!

Good luck with that, Laurent.

ADVICE FROM ANITA LIBERTY

For French boys:

Ya wanna sleep with me?

Try **ASKING**.

Don't get me wrong.....

I'll say no.

But at least both of us will be

clear on what it is you want from me.

And what it is that I'm not gonna put out.

For you.

At least.

Asshole.

(Or is it *L'asshole*?)

LANGUAGE BARRIER

In the beginning . . .
we spoke the same language.
I'm sure we must have,
though it's hard to remember.

And now you're speaking to me
as if I could understand
the words that fall
recklessly out of your mouth.

What are you saying to me?
What are you saying to me?
I'm sorry.
I don't understand.

There are very few things I don't understand.
But, unfortunately, one of them is you.

Les Français left today. It was so sad. Bernard and I have been together since Wednesday. He's a great kisser, although we never went any further than that. He has a great personality, too. I ended up really liking him. Surprisingly. Alexandra and I went home together after school. She was really sad about Thierry, and I acted like I was sadder than I really was about Bernard. Thierry called Alex from the airport and put me on the phone with Bernard. Bernard was really sweet to me and said he'd write me a letter as soon as he got home. He was nice. He didn't rock my world, but he was there, y'know? And that says a lot. I'll probably never see him again. *Tant pis.*

At any rate, these past two weeks have been amazing. Though I don't know exactly what was exchanged (other than a lot of bodily fluids!).

Life is back to normal. Whatever "normal" means in my case. Oh, right—in my case "normal" means "not getting any." Well, it was exciting while it lasted. My mom and dad were on my ass the other night about trying to get involved in some extracurricular activities so I'd have an answer to the question on my college applications about extracurricular activities. I guess writing "Making out with French boys" just won't help me get into the school of my choice. It is something I am particularly good at, however. (And what my parents don't know is that I'm planning on moving to Paris after high school anyway if I don't start getting some action here in the states.) I just don't have that many interests. I'm not athletic. I don't sing. I like reading and I like writing. And those are activities that are included in the academic realm, so it's hard to wear those as a badge of extracurricular honor. Anyway, I decided that I'd join the yearbook committee. It's pretty lax. I'm going to take photographs for them. I borrowed an old camera from my mom and have been experimenting with it around school. So far I have pretty much an entire roll of Adam. I was wandering around with the camera during lunch looking for stuff to photograph, and I came upon Adam and Ben playing guitar on the main stairs. I just started taking pictures, and Adam was smiling at me. Adam! The freakin' cutest and coolest guy in the school. He probably wasn't even smiling at me but just turning it on for the camera. He's a rock star. He can feel the lens on him. It's just instinct for him. It had nothing to do with me. But for one brief shining moment I got to pretend that I was Linda McCartney and he was Paul and that his affection for the camera had nothing to do with being documented and everything to do with the girl behind the lens. (FYI: As a rule I prefer Lennon to McCartney, but the Yoko reference just isn't relevant in this situation.)

PARENTAL INFRACTION (Brief Description)	LEVEL OF ANNOYANCE 1–10 scale: 1 being Easily Forgivable, 10 being Committed to a Nursing Home the Minute They Hit 70
Reading something that was not meant for them to see in the first place and then lecturing me about the content	6
Moving our family to a RODENT-INFESTED unrenovated undivided loft space and then putting me on a PLATFORM in the middle of it	10
Saving a rodent I didn't care about from an untimely (or timely) death	3
Getting on my ass about extra-curricular activities	4 (Would've been 6 except I took off two points since their nagging ultimately led me to being able to photograph the beauty that is Adam)

MY IDOL

Smile fixed for cameras always snapping.
You run your fingers through your light brown hair.
Shiny nose.
Sparkling eyes.
You know so much, yet seem so naive.
How many times have I seen your face
and yearned for your voice?
I feel bonded to you
like the follower of a powerful god.
There have been others.
And maybe soon you, too, will be replaced.

I bear your torch.
I hold your breath.
I am your song.
Always there, always in my mind.
On an endless loop.

    (Sometimes it gets kind of annoying, to be honest.)

hor·ny

(adj.) sexually excited or easily aroused (*slang*)

Anita Liberty was horny. And was more interested in thinking about making out with cute guys than studying for the stupid SATs.

EXCERPT FROM ANITA LIBERTY'S DIARY (AGE 10):

Dear Diary,

My mom and Alexandra and her mom took us to see a play today. In one scene there was a guy hitting another guy over the head with a sausage, and then he put it in front of his pants so it looked like his penis. They had a lot of jokes about penises. I've heard that there are a lot of peep shows and burlesk shows in SoHo. That's downtown New York City. I can't wait till I'm all grown up so I can go see one. I can't imagine what they're like. I've been seeing a lot of sexy stuff lately. I don't know why, but it's just happening a lot. I guess I'm horny (new word). It means that I'm interested in sex. And that I am! I haven't talked to my mom about sex yet, but I will soon. I hope.

I wish I was bigger. Everybody in school makes fun of me and calls me "shrimp" or "chip." I have a lot of things that I would wish for, but I'm still waiting for my very own fairy to come along.

Love,

Anita

I wish there was such a thing as a Future Fairy. I hate not knowing what's going to happen for the rest of my life. I wish I knew that there was some greater plan, some predestined plot, some sort of guidebook. If I just knew that everything was gonna turn out all right, I would be able to relax and not worry so much about everything. If I knew that one day I was going to fall in love with a great guy, get married, have a beautiful daughter, make my living doing something I love, become a household name, everything would be fine. Then I could just sit back and let everything unfold. I hate feeling like my actions are affecting my own destiny. It makes me feel so *responsible*. Like any misstep I take could be my undoing.

Even if the Future Fairy couldn't project her powers very far into the future, that'd be fine too. I'd be happy knowing that if I was talking to a cute guy, she would show up, freeze the action, and tell me if I was wasting my time or not. Even that would be good. But there's no Future Fairy. As always, I'm on my own.

ADAM IS THE MOST WONDERFUL PERSON IN THE WORLD!! He's adorable. Alexandra and I went to a party at Ben's house. I guess she and Ben are back together (she conveniently broke up with him before the French boys landed and then got him back as soon as their plane took off—awfully neat the way she manages that). So since I was hanging around with Alex, and Ben and Adam are buddies, we were sort of a foursome for the night. At some point Adam just sort of started playing with my hand and then giving me these really light, sexy kisses. YAY! He's in a band! He wears ripped jeans! He has long hair! He's a senior! He's cool! Like, not just cool in that I think he's cool. He's cool in a completely objective "that guy is cool" kind of way. And he wants to be with me! Which makes me think that either I'm cool or he's experimenting with dating someone who's not cool. Does the cool guy go after you because you're cooler than you think you are? Or are you cool because you're dating the cool guy? It's sort of like "Which came first, the chicken or the egg?"

However it happened, whether the Earth is off its axis or all of a sudden I'm living in a parallel universe where things I want to happen actually happen . . . he wants to date me. I wanted him to want to date me. He says he doesn't want anything serious, though, so as of now we're only "fooling around." He doesn't call me or act like we're going out at school, but that's fine, 'cause I know we are.

YOU MAKE ME

You make me want to walk on a cliché beach with you,
kiss you in front of the proverbial sunset,
whisper sweet nothings in your ear,
hold your hand and have all kinds of mawkish feelings
well up inside me.

You make me want to sacrifice my originality for you,
give up my inimitability,
abandon my desire for unconventionality,
close the door on my eccentricities.

I know I should be stronger than my feelings for you.
But you make me into the kind of girl who just wants to
be the kind of girl who follows you around and waits for
you after the concert and who feels better about herself
just because she knows that you want to kiss her.

An SAT Word from Anita Liberty

stu·pe·fy
(v.) to astonish

Anita Liberty was stupefied that Adam, unquestionably the coolest guy in school, wanted to make out with her. More than once. And that he actually seemed to be enjoying himself with her during the times when they weren't groping each other hungrily.

ADVICE FROM ANITA LIBERTY

If you find yourself dating the cool guy,
and you're not normally someone who dates cool guys,
enjoy it while it lasts.

Word's getting around school that Adam and I are dating. (Maybe it has something to do with the enormous banner I had printed and hung up in the lunchroom stating that fact. Oh, and the tattoo I had inked onto my forehead.) And my high school stock just shot through the roof. It's like the ultimate endorsement. People who never usually acknowledge my existence are actually smiling at me in the halls and saying hi. It's weird. But great. It's amazing to feel like you're on top of the heap, looking down at all those adoring upturned faces pointed in your direction, saluting you and your ability to attract the alpha male in your pack. It's power. It's sexy. The guy should bottle whatever he's got and sell it. No one would ever feel bad about themselves again. It's like "insta-cool" juice. I actually see a different person when I look in the mirror. I walk taller. I don't think my height is such a problem anymore. I feel witty and relaxed. So, I'm realizing that

that old adage is true, that it *is* actually what's on the inside that counts. However, you gotta feel like *this* on the inside, and how many people get that chance? A rare chosen few of us.

An SAT Math Problem from _Anita Liberty_

Adam is very cool. Anita Liberty is arguably less cool. If they get together, what is the probability that Adam will stay interested in someone who doesn't naturally improve his "cool rank"?

- (A) 100%
- (B) 74%
- (C) 53%
- (D) 14%
- (E) Zilch

(Yo. Idiot. The answer's E.)

71

THE TRUTH AS I SEE IT

I resisted you
for as long as I could.
When I gave in,
it was so good.
You were everything
I wanted you to be.
I wrote the script
and handed you your lines.
How could I not fall in love
with what I had created?
Deep in love with who I wanted you to be.
So completely that I forgot
that we were two people
and that you were still having your own thoughts.
Damn you for having your own thoughts.

Adam and I broke up today. It was the first day back after Christmas break, and that's how this semester started. Wonderful. Happy fucking new year!! I guess I shouldn't have been surprised, given that we'd only been going out for a month and for the last two and a half weeks of that month he was skiing in Vermont and didn't call me once. Anyway, he broke up with me. Although, since we weren't officially going out, I guess "breaking up" wouldn't be the right way to describe the end of whatever it was we had together. The gist is that I don't get to make out with him anymore, and that sucks. He took me to the back stairs during lunch and said that he thought that the relationship was getting too serious. Fine, but I was perfectly prepared for a non-serious relationship, and he's the one who turned it into something more serious. I couldn't help but get more involved. What does he expect? I was really upset this afternoon, but I've calmed down a lot. It wasn't hysteria, like when Laurent dumped me, but I was still pretty sad. I'll see what happens tomorrow. I'm all mixed-up inside. It's like I want to hit him and kiss him. But mostly hit him. Unless he wanted to fool around, and then I'd do that. He was a really good kisser. Fucker.

So far I'm really, really enjoying my junior year.

THIS MODERN-DAY EVE

Although the story goes
that God gave Adam
the job of naming
all that he saw around him,
I believe that Eve
was responsible
for coming up with
some of the more colorful
identifications.
Such as:
Worm.
Dirt.
Mud.
Scum.
Scumbag.
Scum sucker.
Scum-sucking pig.
Scum of the earth.
Motherfucker.
Asshole.
Dick.

An SAT Word from *Anita Liberty*

vit·ri·ol·ic

(adj.) filled with or expressing violent and bitter hatred toward somebody or something

When angry, Anita Liberty goes home and writes vitriolic poetry. You should try it sometime. It really helps to get things off your chest, relieves your feelings of helplessness, allows you to rid yourself of toxic viewpoints. . . . Oh, who am I kidding? It does nothing. I'm still so fucking angry, I could spit.

I just got home from Adam and Ben's concert at school. It was absolute torture. And watching Alexandra watch Ben, and seeing him winking and smiling at her from the stage, made me feel like shit. Adam and Ben were so good, but the whole time I was thinking about how cute Adam is and how much I want him back. And how I had him for like a second. And how great that was. I love him. I do. I really think I do. I can't stand my life without him. I feel so vulnerable. I hate feeling vulnerable.

Oh God, I love him. And the worst part is he knows it.

HIS SENSE OF SELF

He has a healthy EGO.

A really healthy EGO.

His EGO never gets sick.

It may never even get the common cold.

His EGO is impervious to all corruption or compromise.

It stands strong in the face of rejection, disinterest,

and criticism.

Scientists should examine the chemical makeup of his EGO.

It probably holds the secret to immortality.

Or the cure for cancer.

Or the key to world peace.

Or to surviving high school with your dignity intact.

What a dick! A cute dick, but a dick nonetheless. Okay, so, I ran into Adam on the subway home from school yesterday. Bummer any way you cut it. I tried to be aloof, but it was hard. He was so friendly and charming. He oozes it. And I lap it up like vanilla ice cream melting down the side of his cone. He kept giving me these sweet little kisses. On the lips. And holding my hand. He asked me if I was going to the dance at school that night. I wasn't planning on it, but he said he would really like it if I was there. And then he got off the subway, smiling and winking at me the whole time.

So I go home, call Victoria, beg her to meet me at the dance, and I go. I'm a fucking idiot. I get there and Adam's nowhere to be found. Victoria and I hang out for a while being annoyed. Me at Adam. Her at me.

This guy Monty was there. He's pretty cute, I guess. He's a senior and is on the basketball team. But he's the shortest guy on it, so he's closer to my size than Tommy B. Anyway, he kept trying to talk to me and hang out with me. I kept blowing him off because I didn't want Adam to see us together and think I'd moved on.

And then I see *him*. Adam. Man, that guy fucking lights up a room when he walks in. He makes a beeline over to me, gives me a hug and a kiss on the mouth, tells me how glad he is that I decided to come, and then tells me that he has to go find this chick Marissa 'cause his friend told him that she was gonna be there and that she's hot. I was like, *What??!!??* And then he peeled off to look for *Marissa*. Victoria had to nudge me so I could remember to close my mouth.

And then today, when Alexandra and I were talking about the dance, I idly mentioned that Monty was trying to flirt with me and that I didn't want to reciprocate 'cause I didn't want Adam to think that I was interested in Monty. Alexandra asked me, "Why not? Since you saw Adam practically having sex with that girl Marissa right in front of everyone." Gee. No, Alexandra, I actually didn't see that. If I had, I would have been bummed. Kind of like I am now at this very moment as you're telling me this fact in this very fucking nonchalant kind of way like I shouldn't really care when you know, BECAUSE YOU'RE MY FUCKING FRIEND OR SAY YOU ARE ANYWAY, that I've been obsessing about him for the past five and a half weeks. But seriously, thanks for filling me in. She's so spiteful. She seems to really love hurting people. She acts so casual about saying something she knows is going to hurt me. Bitch.

Of course I saw Adam just now as I was heading to biology. (Where I am right now, writing furiously. Mr. Collins thinks I'm taking notes when I'm actually documenting the minutiae of my life—a much worthier pursuit, if you ask me.) I tried to just walk by Adam and ignore him, but he stopped me and gave me that cute fucking sexy little smile of his and said he wanted to talk to me. I said I had a class and didn't want to be late. He asked if maybe we could meet after school. I feigned disinterest and shrugged. Again he smiled his cute fucking sexy little smile and said that he'd meet me out front at 3:35.

Maybe he wants to get back together!! I mean, why else would he be so interested in talking to me? We're already broken up. He seemed so *friendly* and *interested*. Maybe making out with that girl Marissa gave him the perspective he needed and he's realized how great we were together. This is going to be the longest day ever. So far I'm only ten minutes into my first class and I'm dying.

ADVICE FROM ANITA LIBERTY

You're delusional.
get the help you need.
NOW.

Adam and I met up after school. He was flirty and cute and touchy-feely. As always. And I was gearing up for the speech I was sure he was about to deliver—the one where he tells me that he's made a huge mistake letting me go and did I want to be his girlfriend again and, oh, Valentine's Day is coming up and maybe we should go out to dinner and have a really romantic night and could I ever forgive him for not realizing how much I meant to him? And he wants to make sweet love to me in a really gentle and educational and meaningful way since he knows that he'd be my first and he wants it to be really special for me.

EARTH TO ANITA: Come back down here and snap to it. Adam has just told you that he wants to be sure that things are "cool" between you and that he still really likes you and hopes that you can be *friends*. D'ja get that?

ANITA TO EARTH: Yep. I got it. Loud and clear.

HARD FEELINGS

I want to raise your expectations,
then let you down.

I want to ensure that you fail,
emotionally and academically.

I want to steal time from your life.
I want to keep you bored.

I move one day to the next
by thinking of ways to get back at you.

People tell me to let go,
to get over you.
I don't want to get over you
because **I want** you to come
back to me while I'm still angry.
I want to kick you in your sorry face
while you're down kissing my feet.
I don't want to forgive and forget.
I want to hold it against you
for as long as I possibly can
and remember.
I might just have **to kill you**
to put you out of my misery.
Still wanna be friends?

THE THINGS YOU SAY

I'm tired of doing all the talking.
You talk to me for a while.
Tell me what you want from me.
Careful what you say, though.
You can never take it back.

> **Your words will hang**
> **in the air like heavy wet**
> **thunderclouds,**
> **immovable,**
> **dense,**
> **thick in your throat,**
> **filling up your mouth,**
> **stuffed into my ears like cotton.**

So I warn you now.
What you say, I will hold against you.

> **I will wear your words on my skin like intricate tattoos.**

Permanent.
Forever.
Till I die.
Till you die.
I'll never let you forget.
Push my buttons
and I'll play back
our conversations
word for word.
Still wanna be friends?

FREEZING

You didn't resist my rejection.
But you just wanted to make sure that
things are cool between us.
Things are so cool between us
that we don't ever have to speak again.
And you're so full of yourself
that you think I want more.
You're right.
I want more,
but only because what I got
wasn't cool enough.
Still wanna be friends?

WHAT YOU'D DO TO ME

If I were a piece of paper,
you'd fold me up
and mail me back to myself.

If I were a piece of metal,
you'd melt me down
until I had no form at all.

If I were a wallet,
you'd give me back
but keep the cash.

If I were a cricket
you found in your home,
you'd toss me outside,
not caring that crickets
in houses are considered
good luck.

If I were the skyline,
you'd turn away from me,
assuming that I would
always be there
when you wanted to look at me.

87

If I were a car,
you'd total me.

If I were a billboard,
you'd have me saying
"This Space for Rent"
forever.

If I were a chocolate bunny,
you'd bite my head off first
and then gnaw slowly
and clumsily at the rest of my body
until I was an unrecognizable
dark brown mass in your fridge.

Well, I am not a chocolate bunny,
dammit!
I am solid woman.
And I'm not letting you anywhere
near my head,
or my heart,
or my sense of self.

Because I know what you'd do to me
if I let you.
If I let you.
Just don't ever forget
what I could do to you.

88

Let's just say that **if you were** a chocolate bunny, your head isn't the first part I'd bite off. *Still wanna be friends?*

Becauseyou'resofuckingfullofyourself
thatitmakesmesickandyouthinkthatgirls
willalwaysbefallingalloveryouallthe
fuckingtimesoyoudon'thavetoreallyeven
beanicepersonorworkveryhardtomake
surethatyou'llneverbealoneandthat'snot
thefuckingwayitisfortherestofusandIdon't
knowwhyrippedjeansandatightwhiteT-shirt
andlonghairandbeingabletoplaytheguitar
andbeinginabandmakesyousofucking
specialassholeexceptthatitdoesandthat's
oneofthemanyreasonswhyhighschool
sucksassbecausethatsuperficialshit
makesabuttloadofdifferenceanditmakes
mesofuckingangrythatthiswholeincident
wasn'tevenafuckingbliponyoursocial
radarwhenit'stakenupprettymuchallofmy
brainspaceandthat'salotofspacetofillnot
becausemybrainisemptyyouprickbut
becauseit'ssofuckingbigandIwouldreally
liketopunchyouinyourstomach.

Still wanna be friends?
Great. Let's go out for a fucking soda.

90

purge

(v.) to delete unwanted or unneeded data in a
systematic fashion so as to remove all references
to the data

After writing five angry poems about Adam, Anita
Liberty was able to adequately purge herself of any
residual negative (and positive) feelings for that fuck-wad.

It's Valentine's Day. My parents went out. I'm staying home. Like I have a fucking choice. I have no other plans. Of course. I have no reason to celebrate, honor, or even *acknowledge* this holiday. I'm babysitting Hope. Well, actually, I'm kind of "chaperoning" Hope and her *boyfriend*. She's twelve and he's thirteen. They're going to sit on the couch holding hands and watch *The Love Boat*. He bought her flowers and candy and a card. I got jack shit. I got diddly-squat. I got bubkes. I guess someone would actually have to *love* me in order to give me anything for Valentine's Day. Such a stupid holiday. It's a stupi-day. A helliday. A holidon't. Being me on Valentine's Day is like being Jewish on Christmas or Canadian on Thanksgiving or English on the Fourth of July or a slacker on Labor Day. It's just another day, and there's certainly no reason to celebrate it.

VALENTINE'S DAY

I don't believe in valentines.
Flimsy two-dimensional
representations of
devotion.

Easily lost.
Destroyed.
Torn.

Too temporary.
Too fragile.
Too predictable.

If I had a valentine
on Valentine's Day I'd . . .

Never mind. I just got too depressed to finish this poem.
I'm gonna go watch The Love Boat *with two prepubescent*
lovebirds.

PARENTAL INFRACTION (Brief Description)	LEVEL OF ANNOYANCE 1-10 scale, 1 being Easily Forgivable, 10 being Committed to a Nursing Home the Minute They Hit 70
Reading something that was not meant for them to see in the first place and then lecturing me about the content	6
Moving our family to a RODENT-INFESTED unrenovated undivided loft space and then putting me on a PLATFORM in the middle of it	10
Saving a rodent I didn't care about from an untimely (or timely) death	3
Getting on my ass about extra-curricular activities	4 (Would've been 6 except I took off two points since their nagging ultimately led me to being able to photograph the beauty that is Adam)
Making me babysit my younger sister and her "boyfriend" on Valentine's Day	8

I think something's going on with my dad. I was up late studying for the SATs (which are fast approaching), and I heard
him leave and then come back a little while later. It sounded
like he was trying to be quiet, and I think he thought that
everyone was asleep. But I wasn't. I was trying to figure out
what the fuck my father was doing late at night after everyone
was in bed. My fear is that he's smoking again, although I
haven't smelled it on him. He smoked for thirty years. Thirty
years!! And then he stopped. He was really secretive about
stopping, but he went to one of those groups that helps you
quit. He's so not a joiner that it was weird to think of him sitting in meetings and calling people for support whenever he
felt like smoking. But it worked. I was so happy for him when
I finally realized that he'd quit. But now I feel like he's doing
something secretive again and it's freaking me the fuck out.
So much so that I had to stop studying. I was just too stressed
out to concentrate. Well, that and I'm really sleepy.

95

Okay, so tonight I went in to say good night to my dad. He was in his bedroom (or, I should say, *the* bedroom), and as I entered the room, he quickly shoved a magazine into the drawer of his nightstand and closed the drawer. He then acted like he hadn't just done something completely weird. Was my dad looking at porn?!!??? I mean, what other kind of magazine would he be so interested in hiding from me? *The New Yorker?* I don't think so. Eeeew. Gross. Ack. I'm going to be ill. Sick. I said good night (really quickly and without making eye contact) and went back out to my platform-stage bedroom. My mom was in the kitchen, drinking a glass of wine (very out of character for her) and kind of staring off into space. I said I was going to bed. She said good night and went back to her space-staring. I asked if everything was okay. It pained me to do so, 'cause I really wasn't gonna be able to handle any answer but "Of course." But she said "Of course" and smiled and gave me a big hug. Whatever. Parents are weird.

I just woke up to the sound of my parents arguing. So strange. They rarely argue. They're more the make-a-few-nasty-remarks-and-then-quietly-resent-each-other's-very-being types. I'm lying here trying to hear what they're saying and wondering if Hope's awake too. I kind of wish that I could get to her to make sure she's okay. It's so rare that I have the impulse to protect her. I mostly have the impulse to use her as bait to distract whatever's out to get me for long enough so I have time to save myself.

I can't make out much of what they're saying. I thought I just heard my mother telling my father that he was being irresponsible and impulsive. And then I think he said something about how he could do whatever he wanted and he didn't need her permission. They sound really, really mad at each other. I feel bad. But I also feel kind of relieved to have the focus off me for once.

THE SUM OF TWO PARTS

If I am made up of equal parts
of *my mother* and **MY FATHER**,
when **MY FATHER** gets mad at me,
is he getting mad at the part of me
that is himself or the part of me
that is *my mother?*
And when *my mother* is pleased with me,
is she pleased with herself
or pleased with her spouse?
And where the fuck do I fit in?

Here's a hint:

I don't.

PARENTAL INFRACTION (Brief Description)	LEVEL OF ANNOYANCE 1-10 scale, 1 being Easily Forgivable, 10 being Committed to a Nursing Home the Minute They Hit 70
Reading something that was not meant for them to see in the first place and then lecturing me about the content	6
Moving our family to a RODENT-INFESTED unrenovated undivided loft space and then putting me on a PLATFORM in the middle of it	10
Saving a rodent I didn't care about from an untimely (or timely) death	3
Getting on my ass about extra-curricular activities	4 (Would've been 6 except I took off two points since their nagging ultimately led me to being able to photograph the beauty that is Adam)
Making me babysit my younger sister and her "boyfriend" on Valentine's Day	8
Being who they are	11

99

I think Monty likes me.

I think I like Monty.

An SAT Word from <u>Anita Liberty</u>

co·nun·drum

(n.) something puzzling, confusing, or mysterious.

The fact that Anita Liberty decided that she liked Monty at
the exact moment when Monty decided that he liked her,
and that this fact didn't immediately turn Anita's crush on
Monty into contempt for Monty, was a <u>conundrum</u>.

Today Jessica and I were sitting in the library, and Monty came in. We were giggling (okay, maybe not giggling—I don't giggle—but whispering and laughing and goofing around) and talking about how cute he is and how we both sort of had crushes on him. And then, because the Earth spun off its axis for a moment, he walked right over to me and gave me a big kiss. What the hell? I barely know the guy. I mean, I'll take it. I'm not gonna look a gift kiss in the mouth. And it felt great. Not too wet, not too dry. I've become a bit of a kiss connoisseur since I was invaded by the French. I felt a little bad for Jessica, who looked like someone had just flattened her Diet Coke. She'd mentioned that she thought he was cute. But I think he's cute too. And it isn't like she'd mounted a huge campaign to get him to notice her. At least not that I'd noticed. I don't want to do anything to alienate Jessica, but Monty's super-cute and I liked being the focus of his attention. He sat down and we had a really nice talk about college, careers, and other things. He kept putting his hand on my knee and holding my hand and being adorable. Then I said that I had to go to class, so I gave him a small kiss on the cheek, and he pulled me down and gave me like a five-second French kiss. Seriously. Right in the middle of the library. Jessica packed up her stuff and left in a huff. It was sort of embarrassing, but sort of great, too. I'm just glad that girls don't get erections.

Yesterday Monty asked me to go over to his house. So I went. I was incredibly nervous. I really don't know why. Oh, yes I do! Maybe because I'm so fucking inexperienced! And I didn't know what might happen. It was pretty awkward at first, but we went into his bedroom and sat down. He had a lot of bookshelves with lots of books. Good ones. That comforted me. For a minute. Anyway, I sat down on his bed and he sat down next to me. We talked for about ten minutes and then he put his arm around my waist and I lay back and he was kissing me. The light was bothering me so I said "Can you turn off the light? It's in my eyes." He said, "Ah, here's my special feature." And he dimmed the lights. Then he was kissing me again and he put his hand up my shirt! I couldn't believe I let him, but that's not all of it. He sat up after a while and took off his shirt. He said, "I hate clothes." Really? You hate clothes? Or do you mean you just want me to take mine off? On a sudden impulse I took off my shirt too.

Usually I'm extremely modest, but I just wanted to do something to see how it felt. We kept fooling around. It was really nice. Anyway, he tried to unbutton my jeans, but I just went, "Uh-uh." He stopped immediately. I wonder how far he would have gone if I'd let him. I guess all the way. Weird. So weird. I mean, we hardly know each other. Is it all just about biology? Is it all about procreation? What is sex about, anyway? Okay, okay. Obviously it feels good. And we're driven by our hormones. But it just seems so strange to make out with someone you hardly know. Not that I'm a Puritan about it or anything. I was sort of having an out-of-body experience. Honestly, I don't think Monty noticed or cared, as long as my body was there.

ADVICE FROM ANITA LIBERTY

Stop thinking so much.

It's not rocket science.

Just be happy you're finally getting some.

Everyone thinks that Monty and I are going out. And I guess we kinda are. Friday night Monty asked me to go to the basketball game and then over to his house afterward. We arrived, and his mom was there. She was very nice, but I felt completely weird coming in with Monty, meeting her, and then heading immediately upstairs to his room. Obviously, she must have known what we were going to be doing up there. Unless she's a complete idiot. Anyway, upstairs we each sat on separate beds and actually talked for a while. Then he came over to my bed and we lay down. I got up to turn off the lights, and then he unbuttoned my shirt and I unbuttoned his. After a little light making out he unbuttoned and unzipped my jeans. Then he stood up and took off his pants, and I took off mine. I don't know why I'm so ready and willing. Then we got under the covers and he took off his underwear!!! So. There. Wow. Huh. Okay. Well. I have now been in bed with a completely naked boy. *A completely naked boy*. (His penis was huge! But I haven't seen any others, so what do I know? Maybe they're all that big.) I told him that I was getting a little nervous, and he told me there was nothing to be scared of, that he wouldn't do anything I didn't want him to. I tried to give him a hickey, but I don't think it will last until Monday. I like him best when he's gentle and loving, when we're just lying there with his arm around me. Or in the halls hugging me. That's when I can handle this relationship. He goes really quickly. Victoria said that senior boys usually do. I'm scared of what might happen next time. I mean, where do we go from here? Victoria told me to watch it if he tells me he loves me, because that's a classic line of a "user."

Monty told me he loved me.

OH, REALLY? YOU LOVE ME?

What exactly do you mean by that?

You'd run into a burning building, risking your own life, to save mine?

You'd hold back my hair when I'm throwing up?

You'd defend me in a court of law, even if you knew I was in the wrong?

You'd stand up to my parents?

You'd rub my back until I fell asleep?

You'd eat a live bug for me?

You'd hold me while I sobbed in your arms over something trivial?

You'd watch whatever I wanted on television, regardless of what you wanted to watch?

You'd care what I think? About everything?

You'd give me the last cookie on the plate?

You'd spend your time thinking of ways to make me happy?

You'd be nice to my friends?

You'd be cruel to my enemies?

You'd be devoted, kind, sensitive, and emotionally available to me?

You'd never take me to the back stairs and dump me?

What exactly do you mean when you say the words "I love you"?

Do you mean you love me?
Or do you mean you want to fuck me?

I'd put my money on the latter.
But if I'm wrong,
you'd even love my skepticism.

I didn't see Monty until eleven thirty today, and when I did see him, he was pretty cold to me. Jesus! How hard does everything have to be? Maybe he thinks I won't go any further so he doesn't have to bother about me anymore. And maybe he's right. I like him so much, though. I think. I know that I don't want to be dumped by him. Victoria said that maybe since he's graduating in a few months he doesn't want to be attached to anyone. Maybe that's it. I don't know. I just know that I don't want anything to end yet. I'm actually in a relationship that's lasting longer than a week and a half, and I'm interested in seeing how it all plays out. I feel like I'll never get another boyfriend if this doesn't work out. Maybe this is the one chance I get. Unless I move to France. Which is still a distinct possibility.

SHUT DOWN

Putting feelings
into compartments,
drawers,
closets
until later.
What is that?

I feel every feeling
when it comes.
Shouting, *scratching*, **biting** me
in the soft part of my calf.
There's no ignoring them.
They laugh when I snub them.

It's awful.
I wish I was you.
I wish I could shut down.
And you were me . . .
feeling your feelings
all day long every day.

You'd think that sleep would be a reprieve,
but I feel in my dreams, too.
You wouldn't be able to stand it.
    Most of the time, I can't.

en·er·vate

(v.) to weaken, exhaust

Sometimes Anita Liberty found that having a boyfriend enervated her just as much as not having one. Who knew?

Well, I guess everything is back to normal. Monty was just as sweet as could be to me today. I tried to be cold to him in the beginning, but I just couldn't, he looked so gorgeous. He just must not like to have his teammates see me with him. (What is it with these guys and their need to keep their girlfriends closeted? Or is it just me they want to keep closeted? Wow. That's a depressing thought. Throw it on the ever-growing pile that's amassing in my brain.) At any rate, I think we're going out next weekend for our birthdays. How cool is that? That our birthdays are only three days apart? It's like fate. Or coincidence. Or something. I have a ton of schoolwork to do, but it's my birthday and I'll delay if I want to. I have a great picture of Monty and his friend at the basketball game at school last week. I got it printed up, and I'm gonna give it to him for a present. I wonder what he's gonna get for me.

I took the SATs. Or they took me. Not sure which.

My mom and dad went out to a movie tonight, so I snuck into their room and started looking for birthday presents. I'm a practiced snooper. I haven't been surprised by any gifts my family has given to me in years. I can find anything, unwrap it, look at it, and then wrap it up again, and no one's the wiser. Well, there was that one time when my dad bought me a handheld electronic language translator (I'm not sure I can even now figure out what he was thinking when he bought that for me, but it was pretty cool) and I found it and unwrapped it oh-so-carefully. I peeled the Scotch tape and gently unfolded the wrapping paper. I looked at it, played with it for a while (mostly typing in words like "nipple" and "shit" and "penis" to see if it would translate them into French for me—*mamelon* and *merde* and *pénis*—whaddaya know?), then put it back into its box, rewrapped it, making sure that I followed the existing folds of the sparkly gold paper, replaced the tape, retied the ribbon, and returned it carefully to his closet, figuring that he'd never know and I'd act surprised when I opened it on my birthday. That night my dad called me into his room and told me that if I was gonna snoop, I should be better about covering my tracks. In his hand he held the instruction booklet for the handheld electronic language translator. Oops. I'd left it out on my parents' bed. Oh, well. I've gotten better since then. My dad's advice was well taken. I think that was one of the only times.

At any rate, I digress. I looked everywhere. In every closet and dresser drawer. I came up empty-handed. Damn. Maybe they're going to be doing some last-minute shopping. Then I realized that I had forgotten to check my dad's nightstand. I went for it, and only at the last minute did I hesitate when I remembered the night that I came in to him stuffing some magazine into its drawer. Now my interest was twofold—birthday present and covert magazine tastes. I opened the drawer slowly, and what I saw shocked the hell out of me. Was it the latest issue of *Playboy*? *Penthouse*? *Hustler*? *Juggs*? *Big Butts*? Nope. That would have been somewhat normal. Gross, but normal. I was even slightly worried that I might find porn magazines of a different nature. . . . *Just Men*? *Hot Male Review*? *Honcho*? *Hombres Latino*? Blessedly, no. There were magazines in his night-stand all right, but not those kind. I pulled out a copy of *Dog Fancy*, the most recent *Dogs USA*, and the *American Kennel Club Member Newsletter*. Oh my God! This is why my father's been so secretive. This is why they've been fighting. My father is planning on getting me a puppy for my birthday and my mother isn't on board. A puppy!! How cool is that? No wonder I couldn't find anything else. And why would I want to?

PARENTAL COMPENSATION (Brief Description)	LEVEL OF APPRECIATION 1-10 scale: 1 being Moderately Grateful, 10 being You Won't Hear Contempt in My Voice for a Week and I'll Clean My Room Without Being Asked
getting me a puppy for my birthday	10

PARENTAL INFRACTION (Brief Description)	LEVEL OF ANNOYANCE 1-10 scale: 1 being Easily Forgivable, 10 being Committed to a Nursing Home the Minute They Hit 70
Reading something that was not meant for them to see in the first place and then lecturing me about the content	6
Moving our family to a RODENT-INFESTED unrenovated undivided loft space and then putting me on a PLATFORM in the middle of it	10
Saving a rodent I didn't care about from an untimely (or timely) death	3
Getting on my ass about extra-curricular activities	4 (Would've been 6 except I took off two points since their nagging ultimately led me to being able to photograph the beauty that is Adam)
Making me babysit my younger sister and her "boyfriend" on Valentine's Day	8
Being who they are	11

Not getting me a puppy for my birthday	7
getting me a SUMMER ACTING CLASS for my birthday	8

Monty called and said that he wasn't gonna be able to go out with me this weekend 'cause he was sick, but if I wanted to come by after school any day this week and fool around, he'd be psyched. I'm not a germaphobe, but eeew. Dude, just get healthy and then we'll talk. I was sort of interested in having a real "date" with Monty to see what it was like to just hang out with him clothed, but I'm not all that interested in just hanging out at his place again anytime soon. Dunno why.

I saw Monty for the first time in almost two weeks today in school. He got into the school of his choice through early admission, and I guess showing up for the rest of high school just isn't that important to him. He kind of strolls in mid-morning and then leaves after lunch. And I kept missing him. Maybe a little on purpose. At any rate, when I finally saw him, I told him I had a belated birthday present for him, and then (after the briefest hesitation) he said he had one for me, too, but he left it at home so he'd have to give it to me tomorrow. I pulled out the picture of him from my bag and gave it to him. He looked at it and then he hugged me and said, "But this isn't my *real* birthday present, is it? Huh, huh?" and he kept squeezing me tighter. I said, "Well, uh, no, I guess not." So after school I went out and bought him a scarf.

ADVICE FROM ANITA LIBERTY

Okay. You're not an idiot, so I don't know why I have to spell this out for you.

> If a guy you're dating implies that he wants more of a present than the actual present you've just presented him with, he's probably talking about SEX.

Again, I really don't know why I have to constantly explain these things to you. It's so obvious.

WAKE-UP CALL

To sink into you
and *sleep* for a long time.
To lie against you,
breathing,
sleeping,
lost,
free,
where I wanted to be.
Nowhere.
With you.

But you **wake up** first
and leave while my eyes are still closed,
And I **wake up** alone.
Now I'm **wide awake**.
The sun's up and it's in my eyes.
And all of a sudden
I see everything clearly.

You want me to *sleep* with you.
But I realize that that's all I'd be doing with you . . .
Sleeping.
Well, I'm not tired.
I'm on a caffeine high
that might just last for the rest of my life.
And yours.

Monty gave me a light blue enamel silver ring today. The whole thing was wrong. The fact that it was a ring was weird. The fact that it was a *cheap* ring made the fact that it was a ring meaningless. It couldn't have cost more than four dollars, but it's the thought that counts. At least that's what I'm supposed to feel. What I really feel is, *Gee, maybe you could have put, oh, just a tiny bit more thought and a teensy-tiny bit more money into this present you're giving me for our first birthday together since I am supposedly YOUR GIRLFRIEND. Oh, and, supposedly YOU LOVE ME. Jeez.* Anyway, I think he liked the scarf. When I went over to his house last week, I just took off my shirt, but he took off all his clothes!! I guess the guy really doesn't like clothes. And I guess that once you go a certain distance with a guy, there's no turning back. Part of me wants to just get it over with and have my virginity be a thing of the past. But part of me knows that this is something I'm going to remember for the rest of my life and I'd like it to be with someone for whom I had unconflicted feelings. Right now (if the truth be known, and why would I hide the truth?) I'm feeling very tired of Monty. Especially naked Monty.

ADVICE FROM ANITA LIBERTY

When you're thinking about having sex for the first time, think about the story you're gonna have to tell. I mean, for instance (and this is just an example), am I going to tell my future husband or my future children that I lost my virginity to someone whose nickname was Monty? That just sounds ridiculous. If it were me (and it actually is), I'd hold out for a Brad or a Graham or a Patrick or a Carter or an Andrew. All those seem better than . . . Monty.

THINKING BETTER OF HAVING SEX WITH YOU

Buttoned.

Hooked.

Fastened.

Closed.

Zipped.

Don't change.

Leave your clothes on.

I want to remember you this way.

I wish someone could tell me if what I'm feeling (or not feel-ing) for Monty is temporary or something more permanent. I feel like I start to get uncomfortable with a guy, for one reason or another, and then the path from discomfort to contempt is short and slippery. I just feel sort of grossed out by him right now, whereas two weeks ago I felt like I was totally into him. And I just don't know how much of that is because I'm scared of going further with him physically or whether he's just not that interesting to me out of bed. Maybe it's that I only liked the fact that he so clearly liked me. I mean, maybe it was never about him specifically. I feel myself starting to get mean. It's the only way that I can distance myself. I guess this is what happens with guys when they're not into it. Something turns them off or makes them uncomfortable and they react to that by getting cold and distant. I feel myself pulling away from Monty and not really caring about his feelings.

It's just so ironic that when I didn't have a boyfriend, I thought that having one would make life worry-free, but now that I do have one, I have a whole new set of worries. I'm a Pez dispenser of anxiety. Once one anxiety is gone, another one immediately pops up in its place. Oh, god. My life's gonna be hard.

TRYING TO BE NICE

Why is it that no one seems to understand?
Why is it that no one seems to understand
how **hard** it is for me?
Why is it that no one seems to understand
how **hard** it is for me . . .
to be nice?

Courtesy, consideration, gratitude, humility.
These things don't come easily for me.
I have to work at them.
I have to work hard at what other people take for granted.

But people *expect* me to be nice.
They *expect* it.
Like it's nothing out of the ordinary
to be polite.

They only notice when I'm
nasty, **mean**, **bitter**, **contemptuous.**
Proud of myself,
critical of others.

ARROGANT.

People shouldn't notice those qualities.

I was born with those.

Those things come naturally to me.

To see what I see

and to feel better than it—

that's cake.

Being witness to the **inferiority** of my fellow tenants

of this society—

that's not **hard**.

But to respond gently

and humbly and graciously

to the **failings** of humanity.

Now, that is a trick.

I broke up with Monty today. I had been sort of avoiding him for a week or so anyway, so it was just a final-nail-in-the-coffin kind of thing. He seemed really upset. He even got kind of teary-eyed. I did feel bad. I remembered how bad I felt when Adam took me to the back stairs and told me it was over. It sucks. And I can't put my finger on why I'm not interested anymore. I'm just not. I couldn't give him any specifics. But then I was also kind of like, *Hey, y'know, you weren't that attentive and you ran hot and cold on me and you bought me a four-dollar ring at the last minute and you didn't act at all like I was the fucking love of your life either, so what're you so upset about?* I don't know. I sort of liked him better when I was breaking up with him than I had the whole time we were together because he was showing some actual emotion. But I know it was for the best. And he'll be okay. In fact, I saw him leaving school at the end of the day with Jessica. And they were heading in the direction of his home.

I can't say I didn't have a reaction. I felt instantly replaceable. I felt weirdly jealous. I don't want Monty, but that doesn't mean I want anyone else to have him either. And the weird thing is that I know that I could probably snap my fingers and have him back. And that there are girls who do that. Girls who are so vindictive and nasty that they'll keep guys hanging on even when they have no intention of reciprocating their feelings. And they really fuck things up for the rest of us.

ADVICE FROM ANITA LIBERTY

There are a limited number of decent guys in any given high school. If you're one of those girls who tends to attract a lot of guys and you have no intention of using all of them, then cut a few loose so the rest of us can have a go. It's the same lesson we all learned in kindergarten—share, take turns, and don't hog the sand toys.*

*In this case please substitute "hotties" for "sand toys."

nim·bo·stra·tus

(n.) a low, dark layer of rain-bearing cloud covering all of the sky

Despite the fact that Anita Liberty considered herself a wordsmith and skilled writer, she managed to blow the verbal section of the SATs to such an extent that it made her math score look positively outstanding. But Anita Liberty hates math and loves words. Clearly there's something inherently wrong with the way the test is produced if even someone as well-read and well-spoken as Anita Liberty is going to look like she failed. The day that Anita Liberty got the test results and realized that she would need to keep studying and take the test again in the fall in order to get into a decent college, she walked around with a <u>nimbostratus</u> over her head.

PARENTAL COMPENSATION (Brief Description)	LEVEL OF APPRECIATION 1-10 scale: 1 being Moderately Grateful, 10 being You Won't Hear Contempt in My Voice for a Week and I'll Clean My Room Without Being Asked
~~Getting me a puppy for my birthday~~	-10
Not getting on my case about fucking up the SATs and actually being uncharacteristically understanding and reassuring about my having to take them again in the fall	7

My father told me that he wants to take me for a drive next weekend. Just him and me. When I asked why, he said he just wanted to "hang out." I wanted to know why Hope and/or Mom wasn't going along. He said that Hope was going over to a friend's house and that Mom was just . . . busy. He said that he has just been wanting to spend some quality time with me. Uh-huh. Whatever. Nothing sounds like more fun to me than hanging out with my dad in some rental car driving around doin' nothin' and goin' nowhere and spendin' oodles of unmarked hours together. Woo-hoo! Fun times!

I told him that I had to study and that I had plans with friends on either Friday or Saturday night. But he said he'd work around my schedule. What? My father is being accommodating? Something is very, very wrong here.

ADVICE FROM ANITA LIBERTY

When one of your parents casually says that he or
she wants to just "hang out" with you,

don't trust

him or her.

I've put him off as much as I can. My father and I are going somewhere on Sunday morning. And I don't know where. As a rule, I don't like surprises. Especially when they have to do with my parents.

An SAT Word from Anita Liberty

dis·com·fit

(v.) to make somebody feel confused, uneasy, or embarrassed

Anita Liberty's father's desire to spend time alone with Anita and go on some sort of secretive "adventure" with Anita discomfited Anita.

We got a dog today. Which should be good news, but my father was somehow able to fuck this up too. We set out early this morning. My mother gave us an angry yet somewhat resigned look (a look with which I am all too familiar), and we were off. On the way, my father explained to me that when he was a boy, he would find a large cardboard box, ride the bus to the stop nearest the pound, go in, pick out a dog, and bring it back home, much to his mother's dismay. And when one would run away or get hit by a car or get sick and die, my father would go off and replace it immediately. My grandmother always took the dogs in, but never happily. My father said that he had always loved dogs, but his allergies and asthma prevented him from getting one as an adult. However, in doing some *research* (yes, I'm familiar with the contents of your nightstand) he discovered that there were now breeds of dogs that could be termed "hypoallergenic," so he felt that it was time to introduce a new member to the family. And that, obviously, my mother wasn't on board with this decision. Duh. His concession to her was that he wouldn't bring a puppy into the household, but that he would get a dog who was full-grown and already trained. To that end he found a breeder in New Jersey who had a dog who had been used as a "stud" but he wasn't "producing" any show-quality pups so he was being put up for adoption. Great. The dog we were going to retrieve already had marks against him. My dad then went on to talk about his ability to look into a dog's eyes and ascertain the dog's intelligence and adaptability. He said that when we got there, he'd look into the dog's eyes and be able to tell at once whether or not he was the dog for us. If he didn't see a spark of cleverness, we'd just get back into the car and go home. Dogless.

So we finally got there, and the breeder guy takes us to a back room of his (creepy and smelly) house, and there's a dog there. I guess it was a dog. It was really more of a scrawny, hump-backed, shivering, stringy-haired animal cowering in the corner. When we approached the "dog," it darted under a chair with its tail between its legs. I'd seen enough to know that we should, in fact, remain dogless at least another day, but my father actually crouched down on his hands and knees and tried to see into the dog's eyes to check their depth. I couldn't believe my father was still going through with this charade, but he was determined to make eye contact with the trembling creature, and I thought, *Fine. Let him try and then we can go home.* 'Cause although I've always wanted a dog, I've always wanted a *dog*. Something fluffy and cuddly or playful and mischievous. Not whatever it was that was now under an ottoman avoiding my father's persistent gaze.

My father stood up. I turned to go. And then I heard my father say, "We'll take him!"

THE FAMILY DOG

MY FATHER teases him.
My mother protects him.
MY SISTER tries to discipline him.
And I write poems about him.
THE FAMILY DOG.

Rescued from a kennel
only to find himself
caught in a Sisyphean-type
hell.
He's eager to please,
but we all want different things.

MY FATHER wants him to be rowdy.
My mother wants him to be gentle.
MY SISTER wants him to be obedient.
And I want him to understand.
THE FAMILY DOG.

Unable to understand,
he is immobilized by
the variety of our expectations.
He can't tell us what he wants.
He can't express his feelings.
He can't write poetry.
He's just a dog.

But **MY FATHER** wants him to love him best.

My mother wants him to love everyone.

MY SISTER wants him to sit and stay.

And I want him to get out while he can.

THE FAMILY DOG.

ADVICE FROM ANITA LIBERTY

FOR THE FAMILY DOG:

No. Seriously. Listen to me. Get out while you can.

PARENTAL INFRACTION (Brief Description)	LEVEL OF ANNOYANCE 1-10 scale: 1 being Easily Forgivable, 10 being Committed to a Nursing Home the Minute They Hit 70
Reading something that was not meant for them to see in the first place and then lecturing me about the content	6
Moving our family to a RODENT-INFESTED unrenovated undivided loft space and then putting me on a PLATFORM in the middle of it	10
Saving a rodent I didn't care about from an untimely (or timely) death	3
Getting on my ass about extra-curricular activities	4 (Would've been 6 except I took off two points since their nagging ultimately led me to being able to photograph the beauty that is Adam)
Making me babysit my younger sister and her "boyfriend" on Valentine's Day	8
Being who they are	11

Not getting me a puppy for my birthday	7
getting me a SUMMER ACTING CLASS for my birthday	8
getting a crap-ass dog, instead of a cute little puppy	9

School's almost over. It's kind of ending with a whimper, not a bang. I got so blindsided by my SAT score that I ended up actually doing a lot of work for my classes, and it paid off. Who knew that working hard meant that you'd do better in school? Huh. Anyway, my social life has ground to a halt and now it's gonna be summer and all I really have planned are these acting classes that my parents forced on me. Maybe I'll meet a cute guy there. Yeah, right. Who knows what kind of drama-rama-theater-geek-triple-threat freaks I'm gonna encounter? It's a little scary to think about. Maybe if I was going to soccer camp or taking tennis lessons or something, I'd find some cute guy, but I'm not doing those things that cool, sexy boys do. I'm going to acting class, and I don't think the hot guys flock to acting classes during their summer vacations. Maybe I'm wrong. It wouldn't be the first time. Only like the second or third.

An SAT Word from Anita Liberty

am·biv·a·lent

(adj.) having mixed, uncertain, or conflicting feelings
about something

Anita Liberty was ambivalent about . . . pretty much
everything these days.

Alexandra and Ben broke up. I guess he didn't want to be *encumbered* when he went off to college in California. Alexandra's fairly heartbroken. I don't think she's ever been dumped. She's usually the *dumper*. It's a little satisfying to see her pushed off her pedestal for a few minutes, but I do feel bad for her. She seems really sad and vulnerable. She's a beautiful crier too. Of course. She's been really nice to me lately—nothing like vulnerability to make the superior kind to the inferior. We're going to go to the graduation party together. Victoria has no interest in going, and Jessica and I have sort of cooled on each other ever since the whole Monty state of affairs. I'm psyched to go with the newly single Alexandra. We're going to go to her place first and do our makeup and our hair and dress really sexy. She says I can borrow something of hers to wear. Y'know, she can be such a bitch sometimes, but we've been friends for so long that the times when we are able to make a connection, it feels really great. Sort of like having a sister. Oh. Wait. I do have a sister. I forgot for a moment. I guess I meant sort of like having a sister with whom I actually had something in common. Other than genetic material.

I'm so tired. I could really use a cup of coffee. If I drank coffee. Although, what do I have to get up for? I DON'T. Woo-hoo! It's summer vacation and I've got nothing to do today. I'll just stay in my bedroom with the door closed and loll around on my bed doing private things without any interference or interruption from anyone. . . . Or that's what I would do if I had privacy. Or a door.

Last night was interesting. Alexandra was in an excellent mood, for someone who had just been dumped by her boyfriend. I borrowed a sleek little black dress from her. It looked kind of great, if I do say so myself. And Alexandra did a nice job on my makeup and hair. We had bought this mousse on the way to her house. It temporarily changes the color of your hair. She went with dark brown and I chose auburn. Wow, do I love being a redhead. I'm changing it to this color permanently as soon as I'm out of my parents' home. I'm not sure they'd even mind, it looks so good on me. But I wouldn't want to hear about it if they did.

We arrived at the party determined to have a good time. We kissed as many senior boys as we could get our lips on. We'd go up to one and say, "Hey, congratulations on graduating from high school." And then we'd plant one right on his mouth. It was awesome. Monty was there, and when I kissed him, he stuck his tongue into my mouth. I wasn't interested, but I can't blame the guy for trying. Or maybe I can. I thought that he and Jessica had called it quits, but later I saw them making out. I also saw Adam making out with that girl Marissa. I avoided kissing him last night in a rare act of restraint on my part.

Alexandra and I danced a lot together. We were just sort of getting off on being silly and sexy together and knowing that guys were watching us. It was like trying on a costume or a persona. Just acting like you have confidence can make people believe that you are actually confident. (See? I don't need acting classes. I already know what I need to know.)

Ultimately Alexandra bailed on me in favor of making out with Josh, Jessica's older brother, who had come to the party with a couple of his college buddies. Josh is so dreamy. He smiled at me a couple times, but since Jess and I haven't been hanging out that much anymore, I don't think I'm on his radar. Like I ever was. I have no idea why he and his friends were even there. Why would college guys want to come to a high school party—oh, I guess to make out with high school girls. Like Alexandra. But not me. Once again, I went home alone.

I DON'T CARE

I cultivate the *I-don't-care* look
to the point where you
must look at me and think
I really <u>don't</u> care.

But *I do care*.

I want you to think *I don't care*.
But if I really didn't care,
then I would never even
look in the mirror to check
to be sure that it looks
like *I don't care*.

So if you look at me and think *I don't care*,
you might be wrong.
On the other hand, if I look like *I care*,
you might be right.
Or I might just have something stuck in my contact lens.

So my acting classes started today. What a summer. This and re-studying for the SATs. I can barely contain my excitement. I really didn't want to be there, but it's not like I had any other ideas about what to do with my summer, and my parents were so freaking excited by this *genius* idea of theirs.

The first thing I did when I got to the class was size up the boys. The next thing I did was size up my competition. The boys were fairly cute, but I had issues with each of them. One of them was adorable, but he wore designer jeans. Another was super-charismatic but had really bad B.O. Another had movie-star good looks, so he was obviously out of my league. He made Adam look like a troll. Besides, it didn't really matter if the class was made up of superhunky Adonises (Adonae?) with swimmer's bodies—the girls made *me* look like a troll. They were all tan (I burn if I'm out in the sun for more than eleven minutes) and long-legged (I have the legs of a chunky four-year-old) with high cheekbones (Do cheeks have bones?

If so, mine are missing) and long, straight blond hair (My hair isn't straight or blond—I guess the words "frizzy" and "mousy" would be apt in this case, except when I use my super-cool auburn hair mousse and a blow-dryer, but who has time to do *that* every morning?). So whatever. I guess I'll learn to act and leave the flirting and sexy banter to my class-mates. Oh, there was also this guy Gregg who's gonna be a sophomore this year at my school. I've seen him around. He's cute, but too young.

We did some warm-up exercises. Those always make me feel like an idiot. Roaring like a lion. Going boneless like a rag doll. Playing the mirror game. Fuck, this class is gonna

Finally—after a week of messing around and "getting in touch" with our bodies and doing a lot of "exercises"—we did some acting today. We paired up for scenes. I was paired with Designer Jeans. The acting teacher told us that we should always give our character a secret. And I'm like, *Okay, what if my secret is: I have total and complete contempt for this process of pretending to be someone I'm not and then being judged through the narrow scope of your subjective perspective? Hm?* That's a secret. Not a very well-kept secret. Now.

My parents should have gotten me a sweater.

Life is so stupid sometimes. Okay, all the time. We did monologues in class today and the teacher gave us feedback as if we were at a real audition and she was the casting director. We each got "appointments" and then had to show up and act as if we didn't know her, come into the room, introduce ourselves, and do our monologue while the rest of the class watched. It was so stupid. But I called on my newly developed acting skills and hid my contempt. Designer Jeans was terrible. Movie-Star Good Looks was . . . Who cares? He's so hot, he doesn't even have to utter a word to make people pay attention to him. Gregg got up and did an amazing job. He's a really good actor. I actually forgot how much I was sitting there dreading my own "audition" 'cause he was so good. Then I did my "audition." And I think I did pretty well. However, when I was done, the teacher told me that I hadn't shown her enough "colors." What?

A RAINBOW OF RESENTMENT

You said that
I didn't show you enough colors.
I didn't know you wanted to see *colors*.
You want to see *colors*?
I've got *colors*.
Blue is sad.
Green is envious.
Red is angry.
Black is beautiful.
I am all of those things.
(Well, not black on the outside,
but my heart is black with rage.)
I can give you *those* colors.
Maybe those aren't the colors you wanted.
But brown is dull.
Pink is innocent.
Yellow is cowardly.
White is surrender.
You want *those* colors?
Go find yourself another artist.

ADVICE FROM ANITA LIBERTY

Act like you care. It's so much easier. Trust me.

Hope is at sleepaway camp, so home is both more relaxed and more tense at the same time. In some ways it's nice being the only child. In other ways it sucks ass. The focus is all on me now. I hate that. Actually, I love that. Just not when the ones who are focusing on me are my parents.

When I'm not in acting class, I'm out with Victoria or Alexandra. I bought some red cowboy boots that were on sale. They're awesome. They're going to become my signature "look." Everyone will be like, *Ooooh, check out Anita Liberty's cool red cowboy boots. You have to be really confident to pull off wearing* red *cowboy boots.* I also like that they have a heel so it gives me a couple inches. I've never liked wearing skirts and dresses. I only like to wear jeans and . . . well, pretty much just jeans. I've never been into dressing up and being girly. That's my sister's domain. So the idea of high heels doesn't appeal to me. But the cowboy boot, now *there's* an invention. It's too freakin' hot to wear them right now, but I look at them a lot and I'm hoping that it'll be cool enough to wear them on the first day of school. When I'm a *SENIOR*!! Man, I can't wait. Because once I'm a senior, I'm only 160 school days away from graduation and then one summer away from going off to college. If I get in somewhere. If I ace my SATs in the fall. If I get my applications done.

In the meantime I'm stuck at home. Still feeling like a little kid under my parents' roof.

ANITA LIBERTY'S MOM WRITES A POEM

I'm the poet in the family.
The **ONLY** poet in the family.
Or so I thought.

My mother wrote her first poem.
Question: Isn't that nice?
Answer: **NO**.

She asked if I wanted to see it.
I start to say, No, absolutely not, I'm not
interested, I don't care, I won't encourage . . .
and it lands in my lap.

I try not to look down or
move my arms at all.
Maybe a big gust of wind will come along
and just whisk it off my lap.
But I'm not so lucky.
On my lap it stays, and I am stuck.
Stop it! I want to scream.
I'm the only poet in this family.
But I don't.
SCREAM.
Because then she might think I care about what she does.
And I don't.

ADVICE FROM ANITA LIBERTY

Act like you don't care. It's so much easier. Trust me.

PARENTAL INFRACTION (Brief Description)	LEVEL OF ANNOYANCE 1-10 scale: 1 being Easily Forgivable, 10 being Committed to a Nursing Home the Minute They Hit 70
Reading something that was not meant for them to see in the first place and then lecturing me about the content	6
Moving our family to a RODENT-INFESTED unrenovated undivided loft space and then putting me on a PLATFORM in the middle of it	10
Saving a rodent I didn't care about from an untimely (or timely) death	3
Getting on my ass about extra-curricular activities	4 (Would've been 6 except I took off two points since their nagging ultimately led me to being able to photograph the beauty that is Adam)
Making me babysit my younger sister and her "boyfriend" on Valentine's Day	8
Being who they are	11

169

Not getting me a puppy for my birthday	7
Getting me a SUMMER ACTING CLASS for my birthday	8
Getting a crap-ass dog, instead of a cute little puppy	9
Writing a poem about inner personal yearnings and making me read it	6

Movie-Star Good Looks smokes. Fine. I'm not a smoker, but sometimes I'm sorry I'm not. There's such an instant bond that smokers have. It's like their own little cult. Of course smoking is bad for them and they're gonna get sick if they keep it up and probably die a horrible death—blah, blah, blah—but it's like they have a secret society. Today, during a break in our acting class, I stepped outside where Movie-Star Good Looks was having a cigarette. I desperately wanted a reason to talk to him, so I asked if I could "bum" a cigarette. He smiled at me and shook one out of his pack. I took it and he lit it for me. I wonder if he could tell how inexperienced I was. I didn't inhale. It was disgusting. It was a good acting exercise, however, pretending that I wasn't about to throw up. Why does it have to be cigarettes? Why can't it be chocolate? Or hot dogs? Or ginger ale? But at least I got to hang out with the sexiest guy in the class for five uninterrupted minutes. And then we had to go back inside and do our "private activities." The teacher made me sit in a corner and pretend to apply mascara for half an hour. I hope my parents didn't pay a lot for these classes.

We had our final acting class today. Thank god. I really wasn't into it. At all. And everyone else was. In such a big way. I guess acting's not really for me. Unless I can just write all my own material and perform it, and then that wouldn't really be acting, it would just be being me. Anyway, the teacher had asked us to prepare final monologues to do in class. We were supposed to pick something out of a monologue book she had made us buy. I decided to forgo anything I found in the stupid book, and I got up in front of the class and did this instead:

ACTING LIKE I CARE

I don't act to entertain,
but I am an incredible actress.

I never forget my lines,
I'm not easily distracted,
and I can make you believe
whatever I want you to.

I'm such a good actress,
I never stop acting.
I'm always acting.
I act my little heart out.
I could be acting right now. Or not.
You can't tell.
That's how good I am.

I act attentive in math class so **I never** get called on.
I act interested in what my parents say so they'll
stay off my case.
I act like **I don't** care that Adam said **he wasn't** interested in
a relationship and then treated me like we were going out
for two weeks and then dumped me and started having a
relationship with some girl named Marissa so I guess he
was interested in a relationship, just not one with me, and
no, **I'm not** still thinking about it constantly, why would you
think that?

The award has yet to be invented that's
impressive enough to celebrate my work.
(Although I already have my speech written:
A list of people I'd like to publicly humiliate,
because it's so much more fun than giving thanks.)

I am an incredible actress.
And I can prove it.
You probably think I'm as angry as I seem.
I'm not. It's all an act.
I've fooled you.
I'm acting.
I'm not really this angry.

I'm much, much angrier.

ADVICE FROM ANITA LIBERTY

Go with your gut.

Take the risk.

Be brave.

Live your life the way you want to live it.

Just don't expect to be celebrated for it.

Do I actually need to write down the fact that my po-em-monologue didn't go over that well? At least not with the teacher. She never liked me. And the feeling was mutual. There was no big weepy good-bye at the end of class. Everyone just left and went their separate ways. As I was leaving, however, Gregg stopped me and told me that he thought my poem was great. And that he'd love to read more of my work, if I'd let him. He's sweet. Young, but sweet. It was really nice of him to stop me and tell me that he liked my poem. However, it did make me miss saying good-bye to Movie-Star Good Looks. And I know I'll never see him again. Except maybe in my local cine-plex, up on the silver screen. And he'll be really famous and I'll still be me, but I'll be able to tell people that I took an acting class with him and that we were really close friends who sometimes slept together just for fun and that I had to tell him at the end of the summer that we

couldn't continue our illicit affair, at which point he con-
fessed that he'd fallen in love with me and could I please
be his girlfriend, please? And I said no.

Do we all start out feeling special? Chosen? And then watch as others get the lives we thought we were supposed to have? Or is that just me? And have I just embarrassed myself? I have a nice life. I do. I guess. It's just not exactly the life I had in mind. At least not yet. The one I fantasize about. Oh, parts of it are fine. I'm healthy. My parents are tolerable (well, not really, but let's pretend, for a minute, that they are). My sister's not terribly annoying (except for the fact that she seems to be getting more action than I am). But other parts are falling short. I thought I'd be more popular. And cooler. I thought more boys would want me. I thought my friends would be more sophisticated. I thought I'd be richer. I thought I'd be prettier. And taller. And of course the things I don't have are the things I focus on. Because why would I want to focus on the positive aspects of my life when the negative ones are so much more interesting? (And when I use the word "interesting" here, I mean "excruciatingly painful.")

An SAT Word from _Anita Liberty_

cli·max

(n.) the most exciting or important moment or point; a sexual orgasm

Being a senior was inarguably the climax of high school. Anita Liberty was so excited by the thought that it almost gave her a climax. Climax. Climax. Now she can't stop saying the word over and over again 'cause it sounds so weird. Climax. And, honestly, is this word really gonna be on the SATs? 'Cause we all know what we think about when we read or hear this word, and do the SAT people really want us thinking about having an orgasm in the middle of their precious little standardized test? Maybe that's their way of throwing us off. Bastards.

Today was the last first day of high school that I'll ever have!! How sad! Woo-hoo! I'm cryin'! Yee-haw! I'M A SENIOR!!! I wore my new cowboy boots and I got a lot of compliments. I also wore my jeans and a white V-neck T-shirt with my light blue mohair-y sweater tied around my waist. I looked casual and cool and relaxed. Because I am. (Well, except for the "relaxed" part. And the "casual" part. And the "cool" part, depending on who you ask.)

One day down. 159 school days to go.

Alexandra came in today and just announced that she had become a *Wiccan*. First of all, I don't think that's something that you can just decide overnight. I believe (unless I'm wrong, and that's unusual) that Wiccanism is a form of paganism wherein one worships nature and ascribes to the belief that there are multiple deities, both male and female, and engages in rituals at certain times of the year. I've done my research. But whatever. She's decided that she's a teenage witch, and that's all there is to say about that. She's walking around with a book she calls her *Book of Shadows,* and sometimes she stops talking to you mid-sentence, opens it, and starts scribbling in it. She's throwing around a lot of words like "circle of protection" and "pentacle" and "runes." It's all very annoying and contrived and artificial. God, I hate that the most about people in high school, that they're all so unaware of how stupid they're being at any given moment. It's like there should be some giant Mirror of Truth and Alexandra should stand in front of it and it should say, *Cut it out. You're acting like an idiot.* Maybe I should be the Mirror of Truth. And have no friends at all anymore. Alexandra is far too influential in our class. She doesn't need magic powers to turn people against me.

Anyway, she's invited a bunch of us to a séance on Saturday night to contact the spirit of her great-grandmother. Fine. I'm game.

I am the best at what I do.

There's no need to better myself.

No need to improve.

In fact, I'm so far ahead,

I spend my time improving others

just so I can have some friends who are on my level.

Well, almost.

I'm not a magician.

I'm not a witch.

I'm just a senior in high school doing the best I can.

Which, as I hope I've made clear, is **better than most.**

dearth

(n.) a scarcity or lack of something

Anita Liberty was frustrated by the dearth of self-awareness in her fellow classmates, whereas Anita was overflowing with it to the point where she practically had a sense of the activity of each and every molecule that make up her corporeal being and the progression of every thought that forms her intellectual character.

ADVICE FROM ANITA LIBERTY

Think carefully before you do anything extreme.
Like becoming a Wiccan. You're going to have kids
one day. They're going to want to hear about your
high school years. And you're going to have to admit
that you dabbled in witchcraft. And they will never
take you seriously again.

I looked in Alexandra's *Book of Shadows* while she was in the bathroom. Really, it's not my fault. She should have brought it with her. I'm no Wiccan, but I don't think you're supposed to leave your sacred and personal tome around for people to just rifle through. Anyway, I was only able to glance at a page or two, but here's one thing I read:

SPELL 1:
This is to be said whilst looking at the first star at night:

Star light, star bright,
First star I've seen tonight,
I wish I may, I wish I might,
Have the wish I wish tonight.

Okay. So apparently everything you need to know to become

a Wiccan, you learned in nursery school. I wish I'd had time to add this to her book:

SPELL 2:
This is to be said whilst speaking to someone who has said something hurtful:

Sticks and stones
may break my bones.
But names will never
hurt me.

Everyone hates me.

When we got to Alexandra's on Saturday night, she was wearing one of her mother's long black dresses. She had all this dark eye makeup on and red lipstick. She's gone off the deep end. It was all I could do to not laugh out loud. I had brought Victoria along with me, which I could see pissed Alex off. Either that or she was wearing the serious "Wiccan" expression that I'm sure she'd practiced in front of the mirror before we arrived. There were about seven of us there. Alexandra had lit candles and incense, and the place smelled like a brothel, frankly. We sat down in chairs around her parents' dining room table. Alex said we would be starting with the Ouija board. Seriously? The Ouija board? Isn't that like made by Mattel or something? Can't you buy that thing at Toys "R" Us? It's not truly a tool of the occult, is it? What's next? The Magic 8-Ball?

We all put our hands on that plastic spade-shaped thing

marked very clearly with the words "Made in China," and Alexandra closed her eyes and began to sway. She asked a question in a spooky and detached voice, as if she'd gone into some kind of trance. She said, "Oh, Goddess of the Spirit World, hear me. I seek my great-grandmother. Please remove all psychic barriers and allow her to speak through this implement of our mortal world." Then she stopped talking and we all had to concentrate, with our fingers lightly touching the plastic doohickey thing. Slowly, oddly, it started to move. It would pause on certain letters, and Victoria, who was assigned the task of séance secretary since she didn't have an official invite to the "spiritual circle," would write down the letters in the order in which they appeared. Here are the letters that Alexandra's great-grandmother guided us to:

T-H-I-S I-S S-T-U-P-I-D.

I started laughing. I couldn't help myself. It was funny. Everyone looked at me, and then Jenny said that she'd felt me pushing the Ouija hoozywhatsit toward the letters. I denied it, but it was true. I did manipulate the outcome. I just couldn't stand it. I hated the whole pretense of the thing. I hated how serious Alexandra was taking herself. I just wasn't buying it. Then Victoria started laughing too. And then Alexandra told us to leave. We were more than happy to. She also said that I was no longer invited into her "magic circle" and that she was gonna put a hex on me. Ooooh, I'm scared.

An SAT Word from _Anita Liberty_

ve·rac·i·ty
(n.) truthfulness, accuracy

In the interest of _veracity_ Anita Liberty had to admit that she felt smarter than pretty much everybody else. Even those of her classmates who did better than she did on the verbal section of the SATs.

I woke up this morning and I had a huge, ugly pimple right on the center of my nose!! Alexandra's hex worked! She must be a real witch! I had no idea what I was dealing with. I should have been more careful. I shouldn't have been so cavalier. I'M KIDDING!! I have no such pimple on my nose. My skin is pristine. My health is good. I feel great. And totally hex-free!

In school today I found out that there was gonna be a test in French class that I had forgotten to study for, but I ended up knowing all the answers anyway. I lost an earring at lunch but found it attached to my sweater a couple hours later. Tommy B. told me I looked sexy today. Again, it seems that Alexandra's hex was totally ineffective. In fact, it seems to have worked to the opposite extreme—my luck has improved. Maybe that's what happens when you get hexed by an inexperienced witch—she has no idea what she's doing so she ends up casting an auspicious spell on you instead. Thanks, Alex.

Jessica and I made up today. I'm really happy about it. Now that Monty has gone off to college, I guess we both realized that he wasn't worth ruining our friendship over. It's so funny how my friendships with my girlfriends can sometimes mimic a relationship with a boyfriend. Not like I have enough experience in that area in order to draw many conclusions about it, but making up with Jessica was so nice. It felt like we got back together after breaking up. We didn't talk much about the whole situation, but we just agreed that we'd like to start hanging out together again and that we missed each other. Victoria was thrilled, since our "breakup" had been hardest on her in some ways. She likes both of us and didn't want to have to choose sides. The three of us went out to lunch, and it felt great.

I retook the SATs today. Or they retook me. Not sure which.

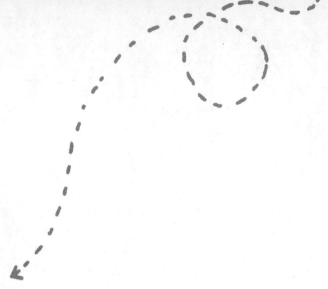

My father sat me down tonight and told me that I need to start working on my college application essays. I said that I had been working on them (a big lie), and he said that he really wants me to get into a good college and that I need to take the application part of the process seriously. To that end, he wants to help me with my personal statement. Uh-huh. So I guess he doesn't quite understand the "personal" part of the personal statement. At any rate, he then launched into his biannual speech about what a good lawyer I'd be. A lawyer? Hello? Is anyone paying attention here? I am not going to be a lawyer. I don't want to be a lawyer. I want to be a poet. I will be a poet. I may have to do something else for money, sure, but I will be a poet.

LAWYERS AND POETS

What's the difference?
To my mind they're **practically** the same thing.
Let me explain.
In both **professions**
reality doesn't have to be
an objective reality
as long as you can **prove** it.

AND I ALWAYS CAN.

I LOOK
FORWARD
TO THE DAY
WHEN MY
DELUSIONS
OF GRANDEUR
ARE REALIZED.

I'M SURE WE
ALL DO.

PARENTAL INFRACTION (Brief Description)	LEVEL OF ANNOYANCE 1-10 scale: 1 being Easily Forgivable, 10 being Committed to a Nursing Home the Minute They Hit 70
Reading something that was not meant for them to see in the first place and then lecturing me about the content	6
Moving our family to a RODENT-INFESTED unrenovated undivided loft space and then putting me on a PLATFORM in the middle of it	10
Saving a rodent I didn't care about from an untimely (or timely) death	3
Getting on my ass about extra-curricular activities	4 (Would've been 6 except I took off two points since their nagging ultimately led me to being able to photograph the beauty that is Adam)
Making me babysit my younger sister and her "boyfriend" on Valentine's Day	8
Being who they are	11

Not getting me a puppy for my birthday	7
Getting me a SUMMER ACTING CLASS for my birthday	8
Getting a crap-ass dog, instead of a cute little puppy	9
Writing a poem about inner personal yearnings and making me read it	6
Suggesting that I go into a profession that has absolutely no relevance to who I am or what I care about	5

WHAT MY PARENTS WANT

"**You shouldn't** be so angry," I hear.

"**You shouldn't** talk back," I hear.

"**You should** work harder, act nicer, be more helpful . . . ,"
I hear.

In my mind I scream back: And you should get a life!
Your own.
This one's mine.
And yet you still feel free to tell me what to wear,

how to behave,

when to be quiet,

what to do next.

Don't worry.
I won't let you down.
I won't bore you.
I won't embarrass you.
That is, not unless you deserve it.
Oh. That's right. **You do.**

HOW CAN I BE WHO I AM AND WHO MY FAMILY WANTS ME TO BE WHEN THE PERSON I AM WOULDN'T BE CAUGHT DEAD WITH THE PERSON MY FAMILY WANTS ME TO BE?

su·per·cil·ious

(adj.) looking down on others; proud and scornful

Anita Liberty decided that, instead of fighting with her father when he insisted that she needed his help to write her "personal" essays for her college applications, she would take advantage of his supercilious nature and manipulate him into actually writing them for her.

ADVICE FROM ANITA LIBERTY

Putting together all those college applications is a lot of work. You have to fill out all those forms, answer all those essay questions, and then write one big essay about something that means something to you. Whatever. Any way you slice it, it just means more work for you. Chances are your parents are worried about you. They're worried that you won't get into the college of your choice. Or their choice. Use that worry to get what you need from them. If one of your parents is a good-enough writer and he's already crawled up your ass about working on your college applications, just slip a pen and paper up there too, and next thing ya know . . . out comes your finished personal essay.

And your pen.

And your father.

If you're lucky.

PARENTAL COMPENSATION (Brief Description)	LEVEL OF APPRECIATION 1-10 scale: 1 being Moderately Grateful, 10 being You Won't Hear Contempt in My Voice for a Week and I'll Clean My Room Without Being Asked
~~Getting me a puppy for my birthday~~	-10
Not getting on my case about fucking up the SATs and actually being uncharacteristically understanding and reassuring about my having to take them again in the fall	7
Writing my personal essay for my college applications so I don't have to	6

My father and I just got into a fight because—You better sit down. Seriously, find a freaking chair and sit down 'cause if you're not sitting down when you read this, you're just gonna fall down on your ass and it's gonna hurt. Okay, good. I'll start again, now that you're safe—My father and I just got into a fight because I PUT POTATO CHIPS ON MY TUNA FISH SALAD SANDWICH. He said that it was disgusting. I told him that it was a good thing he didn't have to eat it. He told me not to talk back. I asked him if maybe he would prefer if I just didn't talk at all and he could just have a running monologue that never ended and he could sell tickets and T-shirts and—oh!—maybe he'd like to book a night on the stage that is my bedroom. He got furious and told me to leave the table. Like I'm a child. I said, "Fine." And I took my deeelicious tuna salad sandwich enhanced with some superthin and crispy potato chips and went to my stage-bedroom. The thing is, my bedroom is about fourteen feet from the dining room table, so I sat there crunching on my sandwich, knowing that every bite was driving a metal spike through my father's overly developed sense of culinary morality.

PARENTAL INFRACTION (Brief Description)	LEVEL OF ANNOYANCE 1-10 scale: 1 being Easily Forgivable, 10 being Committed to a Nursing Home the Minute They Hit 70
Reading something that was not meant for them to see in the first place and then lecturing me about the content	6
Moving our family to a RODENT-INFESTED unrenovated undivided loft space and then putting me on a PLATFORM in the middle of it	10
Saving a rodent I didn't care about from an untimely (or timely) death	3
Getting on my ass about extra-curricular activities	4 (Would've been 6 except I took off two points since their nagging ultimately led me to being able to photograph the beauty that is Adam)
Making me babysit my younger sister and her "boyfriend" on Valentine's Day	8
Being who they are	11

Not getting me a puppy for my birthday	7
Getting me a SUMMER ACTING CLASS for my birthday	8
Getting a crap-ass dog, instead of a cute little puppy	9
Writing a poem about inner personal yearnings and making me read it	6
Suggesting that I go into a profession that has absolutely no relevance to who I am or what I care about	5
Getting mad at me for putting POTATO CHIPS ON MY TUNA FISH SANDWICH	10

I've got news for my parents:

I'M DONE.

This is it.

Time is up and the proctor just told you to

put down your pencils.

Your mail has been sent.

The message has been left.

No more changes can be made.

Not by you, anyway.

You had your turn.

I tried to give you warning

that, at some point, your words would fall on deaf ears.

So here's what you get:

> *I will always leave dishes in the sink*
>
> *until I'm ready to wash them.*
>
> *Even if I run the risk of roaches.*
>
> *I will never make fewer or shorter phone calls.*
>
> *I'm going to continue to tell my friends*
>
> *(and even some strangers)*
>
> *intimate details about my life*
>
> *(and, yes, maybe even yours).*
>
> *I'm going to put my hands in my mouth whenever I want to.*
>
> *Even (maybe especially) in your presence.*
>
> *And if I want to put potato chips on my tuna fish sandwiches,*
>
> *I'll put* **potato chips on my tuna fish sandwiches.**

210

Sorry. Not everything you said to me sank in.

And that's it.

You had your chance to turn me into who you

wanted me to be.

And you didn't succeed.

But don't be too tough on yourselves.

We all make mistakes.

I just refuse to be one of yours.

I did it! I rocked the SATs. Okay, then. I am so relieved. And my parents are beyond relieved. My mother was so happy for me that she said that she would make me whatever I wanted for dinner. I asked for a tuna fish sandwich. And potato chips.

There was a party tonight. Victoria and Jessica and I went. Monty was there, home from college for the Thanksgiving break. I think he was a little wigged when he saw me and Jessica come in together. Adam was also there, with his new college girlfriend. She's gorgeous. And in college. What're ya gonna do? I guess he dumped Marissa. Or not. Who knows with him? Monty seemed pretty drunk and was being a bit of a dick. Being there was seeming like one big fat mistake. I asked Victoria and Jessica if they wanted to leave and just go get a slice. They said yes, so I said I'd go get our coats. I went into the bedroom to retrieve our coats from the enormous coat pile on top of the bed. God, I hate the coat pile. I just loathe it. I hate digging through other people's coats. I hate knowing that other people have dug through mine. I hate finally finding mine on the floor covered in dust (when was the last time these people cleaned?), and I hate the moment when I think I've found my coat but on closer inspection it turns out to be someone else's and I panic that now that person has left wearing my coat and then I actually do find my coat, but it's all very stressful nonetheless. Excuse me, I just got inspired, so I'm interrupting this diary entry for the following poem:

YOU MAKE ME SO HOT

You're good when the weather's bad.
You keep me warm when the temperature drops.
You put yourself around me and
hold me until the cold air is but a memory.
I'd hate winter if it weren't for **you**.

I feel so lucky.
No one should have to go through the winter alone.
Together, we brave the elements.

I feel sorry for those who don't have **you**.
But **you**'re mine.
All mine.
And I won't give **you** up.
No, not ever.

I'll just keep **you** near me
and whisper your name over and over again:
"Parka. Parka. My beautiful black North Face Down Parka."
I love **you**, Parka.

I'm back. Anyway, I'm in the coat room, digging through all these stupid coats, and who should walk in but Monty. I say hi. He says hi. He asks if I'm leaving. I say yes. He sits down on top of the coat pile (exactly the reason that I don't like the coat pile . . . people feel free to sit on it) and he says, "I miss you." And I say, "Uh-huh." And he gets all drunk-serious face and says he wants to take me out to dinner while he's in town. And I sort of don't say anything. And then he pulls me down onto the coat pile and tries to make out with me. He's an ass. I pulled away, found my coat and Victoria's and Jessica's, and left his sorry drunk ass on the coat pile.

I'm not sure it's worth mentioning this to Jessica.

Finally some power. Jessica and I have been selected as this year's co-editors of the yearbook. Watch out, people, there're a couple of new sheriffs in town and things are gonna look a whole lot different around here. We're psyched. We have to raise a lot of money and work hard and make a great yearbook, but we have influence, we have authority, we have titles, we have an office!

We had our first meeting and a bunch of the usual suspects showed up. Geeky freshman, friendless sophomores, extra-curricular-activity-padding juniors. We don't care. I'll take most of the photographs and do most of the graphic design. Jessica's great at organizing people and fund-raising. Her dad works at a big investment firm and he'll get people in his office to contribute to our cause. Also, Jessica's mom belongs to a lot of committees and clubs and she'll get all her fancy friends to take out ads. We're not worried. Also, the faculty adviser assigned to us this year is Mr. Collins. He's a science teacher.

He's the most benign teacher at our school. This is what we think is the running commentary in Mr. Collins's mind as he shuffles through the halls going from his classroom to the science office to the lunchroom to the faculty lounge: "Plants. Plants. Plants. Plants. Plants. Plants. Plants. Plants. Plants. Plants. Plants. Plants. Plants. Plants. Plants. Plants. Plants. Plants. Oh. And plants." We think he gets sexually aroused when he explains photosynthesis. He's gonna be the best faculty adviser ever—he's easily distractable. Anytime he tries to check in on what we're doing and how we're doing it, we'll just wave a shiny little plant in front of his face and he'll lose his train of thought.

ret·ri·bu·tion

(n.) something done to somebody as punishment or vengeance

Anita Liberty wondered if anyone had ever used a high school yearbook as a tool of retribution. And if not, why not? It just seems to make so much sense.

What would it be like to be a complete loser? I mean, I'm not the most popular girl in my class—far from it—but I have friends. And I think I'm at least well-liked (except for the people who hate me). But what about those kids who just have no sense of their place in the high school social hierarchy? Or maybe they do. And maybe that's worse—going through high school and knowing that no one wanted to hang out with you for fear of your "loser-ness" rubbing off? Could you know that you were being actively avoided, that being with you actually made one's social stock plummet, that you were being consistently mocked behind your back and held up as a prime example of "how not to be"? You couldn't know that and go on. There must be some layer of self-protective glaze that coats you and protects you from reality. Otherwise, how else *could* you go on? I try—to an extent—to befriend the people no one wants to befriend. Just to be contrary. Just to show that I don't give a fuck about stupid pre-ordained social dynamics and to show the popular kids that I particularly don't care what *they* think. But sometimes losers are . . . losers. It's the need, the naked need, that really works against them. It's the starving-cat syndrome. If you feed a starving cat, it's just gonna follow you around for the rest of your life looking for another handout. And that gets really overwhelming after a while—the idea that you're the line that holds another being to their very existence. It's too much.

I CAN'T FIX THE WORLD. I CAN ONLY SIT BACK AND CRITICIZE IT.

It's not like I *intentionally* take bad pictures of the people I don't like. It just happens to work out that way. Maybe they're just not photogenic. Maybe my camera is a truth-teller and it's able to capture people's inner truths, such that the photo becomes a picture of their soul and not their body. Jessica and I want everyone to be represented in this yearbook. Our school is small. It shouldn't be a problem. But sometimes we have to choose a picture that's not particularly flattering of someone. And if he's scratching his ass or she's picking her nose or making a really unattractive face, well, it's not our fault. Hey, at least they made it into the yearbook. We're just trying to be fair. And we can't go out of our way to make sure that everyone has a glamour shot. And I'm sure that Mr. Collins would agree. If he actually ever remembered that he's our faculty adviser and that he's supposed to be supervising us and making sure that we're not doing anything that compromises the integrity of the yearbook or could be construed as an abuse of our power. But he's too busy thinking about his pistil and stamen.

I slept over at Jessica's last night. Her parents weren't home so we did layouts for the yearbook while drinking rum-and-Cokes. Dee-licious! I love the rum-and-Coke concoction. I like that it has both caffeine and alcohol, so that you're getting both drunk and wired. It's like you can run a marathon, but not in a straight line. To be honest, it's not a great drink if you're trying to do graphic design, but we're the editors of the fucking yearbook and we're going to lay it out the way we fucking want to lay it out.

Anyway, we were having a great time together and started talking about what a great time we were having together, and then we started talking about how silly it was that we spent so much of the end of last year mad at each other. We hadn't ever really talked about the details of what happened, but fueled by the caffeine and emboldened by the alcohol, we did. She told me how mad she'd been for a while about me dating Monty. I defended myself by saying that they weren't going out at the time and I didn't know how much she liked him, etc. She said she knew all that and that she knew now that she couldn't blame me for dating him. And then we started comparing notes. Apparently, he used all the same moves and lines with her, too. He dimmed the lights for her. He told her he loved her. He'd run sort of hot and cold with her on any given day, just like he did with me. It was basically a replay of my relationship with him—except with sex, which she said was no great shakes. We laughed about how much he seemed to love his own naked body, which is actually an admirable quality (and body), but it made him get up to do a lot of meaningless and trivial things while you were making out with him, just so you'd get a chance to see him in all his glory. He'd adjust the lighting (for the umpteenth time). He'd remember there was a book he wanted to show you. He'd say it was too warm and crack the window. All naked. There was even a bit of what you might call . . . strutting. I mean, sometimes he'd just stand up and walk around and you weren't quite sure why. At one point with Jessica, she thought he was going to start lifting weights naked, but it turned out he was just moving them so he could get to his condom stash.

I then told her about the Thanksgiving party and how he told me he missed me and tried to make out with me on the coat pile. And then she told me that he had cornered *her* as she was coming out of the bathroom and told her he missed *her* and tried to make out with her earlier at that same party. And then we both agreed that not only did the guy *have* a big dick, but he *was* a big dick.

Too much time since I last wrote. I guess I took a break from this as well as from everything else. Christmas break was incredibly, blissfully mellow this year. With my college applications done and gone, I could actually just sort of relax. I've sworn off boys (apparently) for this year and will just sort of bide my time until I get to college (wherever that might be), and I trust that the cute guys will be lining up around the block trying to get a date with me. Yeah, that'll happen.

Jessica and I did do a ton of work on the yearbook over break. I was over at her place a lot. Which was fun, 'cause Josh was there too. At one point he was in the kitchen while we were working on the dining room table and I made sure to talk to Jessica about Alexandra becoming a Wiccan. It didn't seem to evoke any reaction from him, and when he left the room, I asked Jess if anything more had ever happened with him and Alexandra, and she's not even sure he remembers making out with her at the graduation party last year. Excellent.

Oh, come on!! Sherry, whom I've committed to avoiding since she stole a beautiful Parisian right out from under me, came back from Christmas break with an *English accent*. I'll write it again . . . COME ON! She went to England with her family for two weeks, and she's acting like she just picked up this accent naturally. Why, oh why, are people so fucking weird? And why am I always the one who recognizes how weird everything is all the time? It's not a gift, I tell you.

An SAT Math Problem from Anita Liberty

An American teenage girl (we'll call her *Shelly*) goes with her family to England for a period of time. Shelly was born in America. She was raised in America. She's never lived anywhere else but America. Her parents are also American-born and raised. How many days would it take Shelly to naturally assume an English accent?

- (A) 14
- (B) 38
- (C) 97
- (D) 112
- (E) 10–12 years

(I don't know what the answer is, but I know it's *not* A.)

An SAT Word from <u>Anita Liberty</u>

mag·nan·i·mous
(adj.) very generous, kind, or forgiving

Anita Liberty wished that she could be more <u>magnanimous</u>. But it just wasn't in her nature and she had to learn to accept that. And so did everyone else.

I found out today that I got a part in the high school musical. It's *Follies* by Stephen Sondheim and I'm just in the chorus, but I'll be in a lot of numbers and it will be fun and distracting. I sort of tried out on a whim before Christmas break, not thinking that I'd actually get cast. In case you're unfamiliar with the plot of *Follies*, it basically tells the story of these four aging performers as they get together and reminisce about their lives on the night that their old theater is to be destroyed. As the former performers recollect their glory days, the ghosts of their former selves appear in "flashbacks" and the audience sees the history between the characters. Sort of an odd choice for a high school musical, but whatever.

Gregg, my little summer sophomore buddy, got one of the leads. And so did Tommy B. Who knew? He's so gangly, but it turns out that he has a nice voice. And since he's so tall, it gives the impression that he's older. I guess.

What the hell? I left my favorite light blue V-neck sweater in the girls' bathroom on the seventh floor yesterday. I had it tied around my waist and I took it off and left it on a hook in one of the stalls while I peed. I remembered it halfway through history class, but Mr. Singer is such a dick that he won't let anyone leave class to go to the bathroom. So the minute the bell rang, I ran to the bathroom to retrieve it, and it was gone. I remembered that when I was leaving the bathroom, Jenny and Alexandra were walking in, so I found them on the back stairs and asked them if they happened to find my sweater when they went in there. They looked at each other in this fake-innocent kind of way, shrugged, and said no. Fine. Whatever. Then, this morning, Jenny comes in WEARING MY SWEATER. It's my sweater and SHE'S WEARING IT. I got this sweater from my parents for my sixteenth birthday. It has a tiny bit of scalloping on the edge of the V-neck, tiny little eyelet holes throughout, and a tiny bit of mohair, so that there are soft little white hairs running through it. It's really soft and pretty and I LOVE IT. And I wear it a lot. And now Jenny's wearing it. I went up to her and said, "Jenny, that's my sweater." SHE LOOKED RIGHT AT ME AND DENIED IT. What the fuck? I asked her where she got it, then, if not from the girls' bathroom where I LEFT IT. She said her mom bought it for her. Oh, yeah? And how come I've never seen you wear it? She said her mom just got it for her last week. Oh, yeah? And it's already *pilling*? Come on! What is with you people? And there's nothing I can do except continue to argue my point or rip it off her tan, overdeveloped body. And continuing to fight with her about it makes me look like the asshole. How does that work? I just have to sit there in math class and stare at Jenny's big boobs stretching out *MY SWEATER*. I just hate humanity sometimes. Sorry. Scratch that. I hate humanity ALL THE TIME.

Now it's my goal to take the worst picture of Jenny ever and give it its own special page in the yearbook.

Rehearsals for *Follies* have been going well. It's kind of fun, having a place to go, practicing dance steps, hanging out after school, and just generally having a purpose. Gregg has an amazing voice and is an incredible actor (he definitely learned how to give his character a secret this summer). And he's hilarious. He and I have actually become fast friends. We're always goofing around backstage and making fun of other people (one of my favorite pastimes).

Gregg called me at home tonight. We stayed on the phone for two hours, which prompted a lot of dirty looks from my mom and dad. I don't even know what we talked about. It was like talking to Victoria or Jessica. It was just so easy. This weekend we're gonna go to the discount theater ticket stall in Times Square and get cheap tickets to some cheesy Broadway musical. It's gonna be awesome.

And it was. It was awesome. What a day. Gregg and I met uptown at the TKTS booth and got tickets to *A Chorus Line*. He'd already seen it. Twice. But he said he'd be happy to see it again with me. We had some time before the show started, so we walked around and pretended we were tourists. We went into all these overpriced and ridiculous gift shops in Times Square. Gregg bought me a Statue of Liberty lighter. When you push down on her book, her torch produces a flame. It's awesome! We then found a little outdoor public space that was relatively deserted. Gregg produced a pink cigarette from his jacket pocket. Only it wasn't a cigarette, it was a *joint*. I'd never gotten stoned before, and when I told him that, he was shocked. He got the pot from his mother's stash. His mother smokes pot. How cool is that? He asked if I was up for giving it a try. I said I was game and we lit it using my new Statue of Liberty lighter. I didn't know what to expect. He rolled it with strawberry-flavored rolling paper, so it was a little like smoking a LipSmacker lip gloss, but the smoking part was pretty easy. Easier than cigarettes. And being high was fun. It was mellow. And, to me, better than being drunk. I felt more in control and more focused. But I also found everything hilarious and interesting. I just don't understand our society. Why would getting drunk on alcohol be any different from or more acceptable than getting stoned? I just don't get it. Why is there such a stigma attached to marijuana? Everyone wants to feel a little buzzed and have a good time. Unless you're deeply religious or a Puritan or you're abusing your drug of choice. But, seriously, what's the diff? I don't like drinking that much. I don't like the way it makes me feel the next morning. I don't like the feeling of being too out of control. But getting stoned with Gregg was just perfect. I felt giddy and silly, but I woke up feeling fine this morning.

Anyway, *A Chorus Line* was fantastic. I mean, the singing and the dancing and the costumes! It was constantly entertaining. I actually really enjoyed myself. I think I would have even if I hadn't been stoned. Gregg and I got the giggles at one point, and some people in front of us got annoyed, but whatever. Then we went back to Gregg's place. He basically has his own pad 'cause his groovy pot-smokin' mother started dating a guy in the building (Gregg's parents got divorced when he was little) and she stays with him most of the time, so Gregg has the place to himself. Gregg made me a Jarlsberg and cream cheese omelet. It kind of sounds disgusting now, but it was amazing. Like the best food I'd ever eaten. I realized it was getting kind of late, so he walked me downstairs to a cab and I went home.

When I got home, I didn't feel that stoned anymore so I felt comfortable going back to tell my parents I was home and to say good night. My sister was already asleep and my parents were in bed watching TV. My mom asked me if I had a good time on my date. I told her it wasn't a date, that Gregg was just a really good friend who happened to be a guy. My mother then asked me what I thought of the new plant they'd bought that day. When I told her I hadn't noticed a new plant, she looked at me really funny. Whatever. I said I was really tired and was gonna go to bed.

ADVICE FROM ANITA LIBERTY

If you're gonna come home drunk or stoned and you
don't want your parents to know, then make sure
you notice the fucking TREE that is now standing in the
middle of the room you pass through on the way to
their bedroom to say good night to them. 'Cause it's
impossible not to notice the thing. It's a huge, potted,
six-foot-tall palm-tree-type thing. And the only
reason someone could miss it would be if they were
stoned or drunk or blind.

Occasionally something will be conveyed to me by one of my English teachers that's helpful and practical, but I don't generally like the *rules* of writing. Especially the rules that govern poetry. I only like free verse. I don't like to rhyme. I don't like meter. I don't like all the conventions because, well, they're conventional. And that sounds boring. To me it's like painting your own painting or painting by numbers. Sure, if you paint by numbers, you might end up with a painting that looks like you painted it yourself, and you did literally, but you basically just painted where you were told to, and where's the creativity in that?

My teacher, Ms. Braun, just handed back several poems I had written, and she obviously didn't like them. Another way of putting that would be that she just doesn't like me. Because I am what I write. She validated (barely) my creative impulse and my word choice, but she also told me that poetry was actually an art form that had many regulations and restrictions and while it was okay to work outside those parameters at times, poets and writers need to know the rules before they can break them. Blah, blah, BLAH! Whatever, Ms. All-Brawn-and-No-Brains. Maybe you're just not my target audience, my ideal reader, my rabid fan.

I hear what you're saying.

I understand what you're trying to teach me.

I recognize the wisdom of your advice.

And I dismiss it.

POETIC JUSTICE

There are some who say
that what I write is not poetry.
There are some who say
I'm not a real poet.
There are some who say
I don't follow the rules, the structure, the form.

Well,
according to *The Living Webster*
Encyclopedic Dictionary of the
English Language,
poetry is defined as
a written expression
intended to illuminate
aspects of the emotional and
perceptual worlds
inexpressible
in factual writing.
In other words,
one writes poetry to
convey one's feelings.
I'd say that that's exactly what I do.
So here's a special little poem
to express my feelings about
those who say I'm not a real poet:

Kiss my ass, YOU UNIMAGINATIVE MOTHERFUCKERS.

Pretty goddamned poetic,
don't you think?

242

An SAT Word from Anita Liberty

mis·an·thrope

(n.) somebody who hates humankind in general, or dislikes and distrusts other people

I don't need to use this word in a sentence. Somehow I think I'll have no trouble remembering it.

The musical opened tonight. I was nervous. Gregg was fantastic, of course. It went pretty well. My parents and Hope were there. My parents looked really proud of me, more proud of me than they have looked in a long time. And I'm thinking, *Really? You're proud of me? For putting on a leotard and some tights and white gloves and barely keeping up in the dance numbers and just mouthing the words when I'm supposed to sing as part of the chorus and not ever* not *feeling pretty embarrassed for myself?*

Anyway, my parents videotaped it in an uncharacteristic show of parental delight. I'm going to go all corrupt-cop-destroys-the-evidence when I get home and put a magnet near the videotape so it gets erased. I can't have that tape out there for someone to find and blackmail me with in the future. I have to look out for my best interests. If I don't do it, who will?

The closing party for the musical was tonight. I just got home. I'm still buzzed. But not 'cause I was drinking. And not 'cause I was stoned. I MADE OUT WITH GREGG. Like all night. It was amazing. I had a vague sense that people were walking by and staring at us, but I didn't care. He's an amazing kisser. It just felt so normal and so right. We've been spending so much time together and it's been so easy. I never stress about anything when I'm with him. He makes me feel so comfortable. It truly is like being with my best friend. Only he's a boy. And I get to make out with him. We had been making out for a while and we finally came up for air, and he looked at me and said, "So?" We laughed really hard. And it wasn't that funny. Wow. I really never knew it could be like this. I'm really kind of floating. It's a strange feeling. I feel giddy, but grounded at the same time.

Oh, what a day! I couldn't wait to see Gregg in school today. I walked in and immediately started looking for him. It wasn't like with other guys I've been interested in, where I have to play it cool and act casual and pretend that I'm less committed than I am. Maybe it's the difference in our ages that makes me so sure of his feelings for me. Maybe it's the fact that we were friends first or that I never considered him a real *boyfriend* prospect until the moment we kissed. Whatever the reason, I love this feeling. I hope it never ends. I love feeling secure. I love being able to express my emotions freely and not second-guess myself all the time.

I will say that I felt like the center of attention at school. Everyone who was at the closing-night party was looking at me, since Gregg and I had basically been pawing each other all night out in the open. And pretty much everyone else at school who hadn't been at the party had *heard* about the party from someone who had been at the party. Maybe I was being paranoid or hypersensitive or maybe even self-centered, but it really seemed that everyone's eyes were on me and that everyone was talking and whispering and gossiping about me and Gregg.

I finally saw Gregg after second period. I grabbed him, took him to an empty classroom, and, before he could say anything, I just started kissing him passionately. When we stopped to breathe, he was grinning. He told me to meet him at lunch and we'd go get something to eat.

He met me in the lobby and took my hand (he's really bold for a sophomore boy, and I'm kind of loving that), and we walked out of school holding hands. It was one of the first days that felt like spring. Birds were chirping, the sun was shining, buds were blooming. I'm not kidding. We picked up some sandwiches to go. I asked where we were going, and Gregg said that it was a surprise. He brought me to his dad's apartment, which is around the corner from school. His dad works in Manhattan so he's not home during the day. We had forty-five minutes until we both had to get back to school for our next class. We made out for forty-two minutes straight. We never touched our sandwiches and had to run back to school so we weren't late.

Again, everyone looked at us as we came in. And I really, really, really couldn't have cared less what any one of them was thinking.

I'm on a cloud. A rose-colored one. Not the *nimbostratus* that I'm usually under.

An SAT Math Problem from *Anita Liberty*

Gregg + Anita + Gregg's dad's apartment − Gregg's dad × forty-five minutes ÷ an intense mutual attraction =

- Ⓐ A make-out session
- Ⓑ A hot make-out session
- Ⓒ A super-hot make-out session
- Ⓓ A super-duper-hot make-out session
- Ⓔ The most super-duper, hottest, sexiest make-out session ever in the history of make-out sessions

(I don't have to tell you the answer to this one, do I?)

Pol·ly·an·na

(n.) a person characterized by irrepressible optimism
and a tendency to find good in everything

Anita Liberty knew that she could never truly consider
herself a <u>Pollyanna</u>, as her cynicism and anger ran
too deep, but her outlook had certainly changed since
yesterday.

I never knew that it could start with friendship
and end with love.

I never knew that being in love
could actually be this easy.

I never knew that it would end up being
less stressful to be with you than without you.

I never knew that being naked with another person
could feel so normal.

I never knew I could laugh so hard.

I never knew that I could be myself with a boy.

I never knew that just being me would be enough.

I never knew that we'd have so much in common
and that we'd discover so many things we'd never done
before alone that we liked to do together.

I never knew that it was going to be you.
And that everyone else who came before you was just practice.

I never knew.

But if I had, would anything have played out differently?

We'll never know.

And, thankfully, we'll never have to.

For some reason when I first introduced the idea of sleeping over at Gregg's apartment, my parents said yes. They barely even looked up. It's like they didn't hear me or understand what it was I was asking. My mom idly asked if his mom was gonna be home, but when I lied and said yes, she totally believed me and said it was fine. My dad asked what we were gonna do, and I said, "French," which implied French home-work, but I quite enjoyed the double *entendre*. Sometimes it's just about amusing myself.

Things with Gregg are going great. And, I don't know why, but I haven't been that interested in documenting. I guess happiness is not conducive to writing. It's certainly not as much fun as writing when I'm angry about something. But fooling around with a cute guy is preferable to writing under any circumstance, so I guess it all comes out in the wash.

People at school are still scandalized by Gregg's and my relationship. It's so stupid. I guess people are jealous. Or maybe it's the fact that he's two grades below me. It's just so interesting how the gossip doesn't even faze me because I have no doubts about how Gregg and I feel about each other.

TALK

Talk, talk, talk, talk, talk, talk, talk, talk, talk, talk, talk, talk, talk, talk,
talk, talk, talk, talk, talk, talk, talk, talk, talk, talk, talk, talk, talk, talk,
talk, talk, talk, talk, talk, talk, talk, talk, talk, talk, talk, talk, talk, talk,
talk, talk, talk, talk, talk, talk, talk, talk, talk, talk, talk, talk, talk, talk,
talk, talk, talk, talk, talk, talk, talk, talk, talk, talk, talk, talk, talk.
Do you even hear your own voices?
Do you know how silly you sound?
Do you realize how boring you are?
Talk, talk.
Keep talking.
Enjoy yourselves.
I want you to talk.
I want you to get it out of your systems.
Talk, talk, talk, talk, talk, talk, talk, talk, talk, talk, talk, talk, talk, talk,
talk, talk, talk, talk, talk, talk, talk, talk, talk, talk, talk, talk, talk, talk,
talk, talk, talk, talk, talk, talk, talk, talk, talk, talk, talk, talk, talk, talk,
talk, talk, talk, talk, talk, talk, talk, talk, talk, talk, talk, talk, talk, talk,
talk, talk, talk, talk, talk, talk, talk, talk, talk, talk, talk, talk, talk, talk.
Envy or spite?
Go ahead. Pick one.
And talk.
Maybe if you could use your eyes instead of your mouths,
you would see how much your talk doesn't affect me,
how much I couldn't care less when you
talk, talk, talk, talk, talk, talk, talk, talk, talk, talk, talk, talk, talk, talk, talk,
talk, talk, talk, talk, talk, talk, talk, talk, talk, talk, talk, talk, talk, talk, talk,

talk, talk, talk, talk, talk, talk, talk, talk, talk, talk, talk, talk, talk, talk, talk,
talk, talk, talk, talk, talk, talk, talk, talk, talk, talk, talk, talk, talk, talk, talk,
talk, talk, talk, talk, talk, talk, talk, talk, talk, talk, talk, talk, talk, talk, talk,
talk, talk, talk, talk, talk, talk, talk, talk, talk, talk, talk, talk, talk, talk, talk,
talk, talk, talk, talk, talk, talk, talk, talk, talk, talk, talk, talk, talk, talk, talk,
talk, talk, talk, talk, talk, talk, talk, talk, talk, talk, talk, talk, talk, talk, talk,
talk, talk, talk, talk, talk, talk, talk, talk, talk, talk, talk, talk, talk, talk, talk,
talk, talk, talk, talk, talk, talk, talk, talk, talk, talk, talk, talk, talk, talk, talk,
talk, talk, talk, talk, talk, talk, talk, talk, talk, talk, talk, talk, talk, talk, talk,
talk, talk, talk, talk, talk, talk, talk, talk, talk, talk, talk, talk, talk, talk, talk,
talk, talk, talk, talk, talk, talk, talk, talk, talk, talk, talk, talk, talk, talk, talk,
talk, talk, talk, talk, talk, talk, talk, talk, talk, talk, talk, talk, talk, talk, talk,
talk, talk, talk, talk, talk, talk, talk, talk, talk, talk, talk, talk, talk, talk, talk,
talk, talk, talk, talk, talk, talk, talk, talk, talk, talk, talk, talk, talk, talk, talk,
talk, talk, talk, talk, talk, talk, talk, talk, talk, talk, talk, talk, talk, talk, talk,
talk, talk, talk, talk, talk, talk, talk, talk, talk, talk, talk, talk, talk, talk, talk,
talk, talk, talk, talk, talk, talk, talk, talk, talk, talk, talk, talk, talk, talk, talk,
talk, talk, talk, talk, talk, talk, talk, talk, talk, talk, talk, talk, talk, talk, talk,
talk, talk, talk, talk, talk, talk, talk, talk, talk, talk, talk, talk, talk, talk, talk,
talk, talk, talk, talk, talk, talk, talk, talk, talk, talk, talk, talk, talk, talk, talk,
talk, talk, talk, talk, talk, talk, talk, talk, talk, talk, talk, talk, talk, talk, talk,
talk, talk, talk, talk, talk, talk, talk, talk, talk, talk, talk, talk, talk, talk, talk,
talk, talk, talk, talk, talk, talk, talk, talk, talk, talk, talk, talk, talk, talk, talk,
talk, talk, talk, talk, talk, talk, talk, talk, talk, talk, talk, talk, talk, talk, talk,
talk, talk, talk, talk, talk, talk, talk, talk, talk, talk, talk, talk, talk, talk, talk,
talk, talk, talk, talk, talk, talk, talk, talk, talk, talk, talk, talk, talk, talk, talk,
talk, talk, talk, talk, talk, talk, talk, talk, talk, talk, talk, talk, talk, talk, talk,
talk, talk, talk, talk, talk, talk, talk, talk, talk, talk, talk, talk, talk, talk, talk,
talk, talk, talk, talk, talk, talk, talk, talk, talk, talk, talk, talk, talk, talk, talk.

My parents must still be under the impression that Gregg and I are just friends, and I have to say, it makes everything so much easier. They still have no problem with me staying over at his place. They don't even ask whether his mother is gonna be there anymore. I don't know why they're not picking up on the obvious sexual tension between us, but they're not. And they're just completely laid back and unquestioning about my spending time with him. It's so weird for them. They can get fucking crazy about the littlest thing, and then they're completely oblivious to the fact that I have a boyfriend. I mean, Gregg's a really sweet guy and we did start out as friends, so maybe they think that's still all we are, but Gregg *is* a boy and he does have a penis and one would think that they might be more concerned about the proximity of that penis to their daughter's vagina. 'Cause it's getting closer every day.

PARENTAL COMPENSATION (Brief Description)	LEVEL OF APPRECIATION 1-10 scale: 1 being Moderately Grateful, 10 being You Won't Hear Contempt in My Voice for a Week and I'll Clean My Room Without Being Asked
~~Getting me a puppy for my birthday~~	-10
Not getting on my case about fucking up the SATs and actually being uncharacteristically understanding and reassuring about my having to take them again in the fall	7
Writing my personal essay for my college applications so I don't have to	6
Overlooking the fact that my platonic relationship with Gregg has turned into an extremely non-platonic one, thus letting me sleep over with him and spend as much time as I want with him without questioning my every move	14

MY EIGHTEENTH BIRTHDAY

I woke up.

My mom made pancakes.

My sister gave me earrings.

My dad bought me flowers.

I went to school.

I got a nice card from Victoria.

I aced the math test.

I went home with Gregg after school.

We had sex.

We ate cake.

I went home.

I went out to dinner with my family.

I went to bed.

In case you missed that . . .

I HAD SEX!!!

At my birthday dinner with my parents and my sister, I kept thinking that if all of a sudden a big green light appeared over the heads of everyone who was *not* a virgin, a big green light would appear over my head. And wouldn't my parents be shocked.

Ironically, at the same moment that I was having this thought my mother leaned over to me and said conspiratorially, "Eighteen. Wow. I guess it's time that we had a talk." Nice timing, Mom.

Fakespeare

Love, for me, was never so true.

Whilst before it felt as if mine heart did sleep.

Your touch has woken it from its slumber deep.

And made it beat for not only one, but two.

My heart stretches its wings as if they were new.

May you knowst my love is yours to keep.

When we are apart, my heart doest weep.

As it desires the next time when we can screw.

Heart, now alert, let not thou sleep again.

Until the day comes when you turn away.

It cuts me like a dagger to think of that day.

May it never come and cause us great pain.

I darest not think our love ever will wane.

For always my heart, my self, will stay open for you.

ADVICE FROM ANITA LIBERTY

Don't try writing poetry when you're happy.

It's not gonna turn out well.

In fact, it might suck.

Just put your pen down and go get laid.

You'll be doing all of us a favor.

Funny how all I wanted was to get into a good college and leave high school behind and move out of my parents' home and start living my real life. I was waiting and waiting for that moment. And now it has arrived. I got into a good college. My dad's personal statement must have worked. I guess he knows me better than I know myself. Scary thought. And now I have a letter of acceptance from a great school in Massachusetts. Actually, the same school that Jessica's brother Josh is attending. It was my first choice. Not that that's the reason *why* it was my first choice. And not that the fact that he goes there matters at all anymore now that I'm with Gregg. I should be happy, but I'm miserable. I don't want to leave Gregg behind. He has two more years of high school and I hate the thought of not being able to see him every day. And I really hate the thought of not being able to have sex with him. I really love sex. I'm so glad that we were each other's firsts. God, it's fun. It gets more fun the more you do it too. I pretty much want to be doing it all the time when we're alone together. I make Gregg take me home to his dad's place during lunchtime so we can have sex in the middle of the day. Every day. But the other day Gregg told me that sometimes he'd like to have lunch at lunch. What's that about? Food rather than sex? Not even a choice. I would say I'm definitely the aggressor in this relationship, especially sexually. He's much more tentative and seems even to be holding back sometimes. Maybe it's 'cause he's younger and that's still an issue for him even though it's not at all for me. He's just not your stereotypical guy when it comes to sex. He's amazing in bed and totally present while we're doing it, but he seems just as happy cuddling and kissing. Now that I've experienced sex, I just want to go all the way all the time. Oh, if Jean-François, Laurent, Monty, and Adam knew what they were missing! Suckahs!

A COMPLETELY HYPOTHETICAL SITUATION
PRESENTED BY ANITA LIBERTY
(TO BE SEEN BY NO ONE AT NO TIME EVER)

So, say you were co-editor of the yearbook your senior year of high school and you raised a lot of money. I mean, *a lot* of money. And you were able to produce the most kick-ass yearbook your school had ever had. By a long shot. And you still didn't even come close to spending all the money you'd raised. You ordered the most expensive cover. You got the most expensive embossing. You used silver lettering on the front, which cost extra. It looked really professional and well done. Everyone was seriously pleased. Which was good, 'cause you and your co-editor worked your asses off on this thing. It was a hell of a lot more work than you were prepared for, and you had to apply to colleges at the same time and get good grades, and you had sex for the first time in the middle of everything, and that was good, but time-consuming, 'cause once you started having sex, you kind of never wanted to stop, so any free time you had was eaten up by that pursuit. At any rate, there you were, sitting on this huge amount of money. Of course, you and your co-editor planned to leave it for next year's yearbook committee, but, honestly, they could have just used the money you had leftover from your yearbook and done a whole 'nother yearbook with it. And how would that be fair? How would that teach them anything about what it means to raise money and allocate funds in order to produce a keepsake for your school?

265

Given all that I've told you, wouldn't you say it was reasonable, *rational* even, for the co-editors to take some of that money—a tiny amount, really—and buy themselves each a suede jacket? Sure! Why not? And, also, don't you think it sounds practical that one of the coeditors should also use some of that money to buy her diaphragm at Planned Parenthood? 'Cause condoms are so, y'know, *impersonal*, once you've been having sex with the same person for a while and you plan to continue to have sex with that same person for a while and neither of you has had sex with anyone else so you know you're free of any and all sexually transmitted diseases? And bringing up the matter with one's mother would just be opening a whole can of worms?

I mean, really, who's this hurting? No one.

Who's this helping? No one. (Remember, this is just a *hypothetical* situation.)

Okay, then. The moment I've been waiting for since I was twelve. The last day of high school. Ever. I'm done. Done, done, done. I've always loved the last day of school, but this was amazing. The last day is always such a weird day. Everything is in disarray. Everyone's throwing stuff out, cleaning out their lockers, dumping their unwanted shit. It's like kids have taken over the institution and they have no respect for the hallowed halls of academia. It's fantastic! It's *Lord of the Flies*!! (Where's Piggy? I want to kill him with a sharp stick.) There's this collective feeling of freedom and exuberance in a place that's usually so freaking depressing. I love the noise level, the mess, the contrast between this day and every other day of the year. All rules are suspended. Even the teachers seem joyful and relieved. If high school were like this every day, it might be tolerable.

I have to say that as happy as I was to experience this last day, it was also weird. Different. There's a bit of melancholy mixed in among the euphoria. There just is. This has been my home away from home for twelve years. I've been going to this same school, this same building, since my first day of first grade. Endings are hard for me. They always have been. I've never really liked change. Even when it's for the best. I know I'll stay in touch with my very best friends, but it is hard to think about saying good-bye to all the supporting players—the people who I see day in and day out, who I might have lunch with now and then or study with once in a while or make out with on occasion—the ones who will be making their final exit from my life. (At least until our tenth reunion, when I come back famous and tan and redheaded and everyone, in awe of my success, my celebrity, and my beauty, flocks to me like moths to a flame.)

Everyone loved the yearbook. *Loved it.* I overheard a lot of people idly complaining about their own pictures, but no one ever likes the way he or she looks in photographs. That's not our fault. (Rather, it was our *intention.*) As a whole the book was incredibly well received. Mr. Collins looked proud of himself. He's either taking credit he doesn't deserve for overseeing the yearbook production or he might just have read an article about the discovery of a new variety of fungus in the Costa Rican rain forest. Can't be sure.

Gregg and I walked around holding hands all day. Obviously, today wasn't the same for him as it was for me. That made me a little sad. But I love him and know that we're going to be able to transcend all of this bullshit and keep our relationship going once I go off to college.

One reason people were being particularly nice to me (other than appreciation for my contribution to the best yearbook ever produced) was the fact that I'm having a graduation party! Yep. My parents told me that I could have a graduation party at our loft. They're not worried about me and my friends trashing the place since they're gonna renovate it right after I leave for college anyway. Of course. They're going to make it cool and beautiful and sexy as soon as I'm not there to appreciate it, but whatever. The point is that I'm having a rockin' Manhattan loft party and I'm in charge of the guest list!

PARENTAL COMPENSATION (Brief Description)	LEVEL OF APPRECIATION 1-10 scale: 1 being Moderately Grateful, 10 being You Won't Hear Contempt in My Voice for a Week and I'll Clean My Room Without Being Asked)
~~Getting me a puppy for my birthday~~	-10
Not getting on my case about fucking up the SATs and actually being uncharacteristically understanding and reassuring about my having to take them again in the fall	7
Writing my personal essay for my college applications so I don't have to	6
Overlooking the fact that my platonic relationship with Gregg has turned into an extremely nonplatonic one, thus letting me sleep over with him and spend as much time as I want with him without questioning my every move	14

Letting me have a graduation party at their unrenovated undivided loft space	10

WHY IT'S A GOOD THING MY CLASSMATES DIDN'T ASK ME TO SPEAK AT OUR GRADUATION, 'CAUSE THIS IS THE SPEECH I WOULD HAVE GIVEN

High school is crap. That's right. You heard me. Crap. I mean, sure, you learn stuff and you make friends and whatever, but all the pretense, the attitudes, the posturing that goes on during the course of every day—it's all *bullshit*.

I can't stand the miscommunications of daily life due to the fact that people can't be direct. I want to tell people what I think of them. I want to hear what people say behind *my* back. I want to express my thoughts and feelings directly and unapologetically. I don't want to have to beat around the bush. Or pretend that something doesn't bother me when it does. I just think life would be so much better if people could dispense with the little trickeries and ploys and artificial behavior that make up so much of the social dynamics of high school. And I'm sure there are a lot of you out there today who would agree with me. If you had the freedom to be honest.

What would it be like if people could just be honest? With themselves and one another? If people could just come out and say what they want and what they need instead of hiding their feelings or being cryptic about their desires? What I mean is, if I like someone, I should just be able to come right out and say, "Gee, I like you. Maybe we can hang out alone sometime, and if it's fun, then we can spend more time together and start touching each other in a non-platonic way and see how that goes and so on and so on and so on until it gets not fun or boring, and then I'll let you know that and we can move on with our lives." Or if someone likes me, he could just say, "I like you, but if we start fooling around, I'm gonna want to have sex and if you're not ready for that, then I'm gonna move on to someone who will have sex with me, okay?" It would just make things so clear. And clarity is something that I, for one, found sorely lacking in high school.

This goes for friendships, too. I know that people say nasty things about me when I'm not there. It's inevitable. You don't have to feel bad about it. I can't be everybody's favorite person all the time. I know that. But there have been times when I've walked into rooms and the minute I arrive people stop talking and look at me guiltily. Obviously, people are welcome to have conversations that don't include me, but if they *are* talking about me, then just fucking come out and say it and at least give me a chance to respond. I want to at least have the chance to defend myself from people's misinterpretations of my behavior. I don't need everyone to like me, and I certainly don't like everyone, but let's just be civil and acknowledge our feelings of contempt or jealousy or superiority or disgust or anger and learn how to peaceably hate each other.

Even our teachers adhere to the roles they feel they're supposed to be playing. You teachers out there know what I'm talking about. I realize that sometimes the work I handed in was unconventional or didn't necessarily follow an assignment to the very letter, but is that so bad? Shouldn't I be rewarded for my courage in breaking from the herd? Isn't being an individual with a unique voice something that society should be celebrating? Even if that voice is saying something you didn't necessarily ask to hear? Or *want* to hear? Or *feel comfortable* hearing?

And if the world worked the way I believe it should, then when my mother was bugging me about something irrelevant, I could just say, "Come on, Mom. Is this really something that you want to get into a fight about, or are you just on my ass because you're in a bad mood and you feel justified in taking it out on me because I'm your child and you're my parent and you have automatic and irrevocable (until I'm eighteen) authority?"

I'm not saying that I'm going to get to a place where I'll be able to influence the way the world works. (That would be an arrogant declaration coming from someone on the eve of receiving her high school diploma.) I'm not saying that I have all the answers or that I know everything. (Although I frequently *think* that, I wouldn't say it out loud.) What I am saying is that maybe our little high school universe would be a better place to live for four years if, along with math and science and English and history and French and music, we were required to learn how to talk about our emotions, express our intimate yearnings, and say what we mean without feeling ashamed or embarrassed. Those would be useful tools to have in the real world. I'm going to spend a lot of my life honing mine. I'd advise you, my friends and my enemies, to spend some time honing yours.

I didn't like all of you. I loved a couple of you. I hated some of you. Most of you irritated me. A few of you impressed me. If you want to know which category you're in, see me after the graduation ceremony and I'll tell you the truth. In fact, it would be my pleasure.

I have about two seconds to write. I'm about to leave for my *high school graduation*. I'm dressed and ready to go. I'm wearing pants. I know most of the girls in my class are gonna be wearing dresses or skirts, but there's no dress code and we don't wear graduation gowns, so it really is a moment to do whatever you want. And I'm wearing exactly what I want. My mom took me shopping a couple weeks ago and bought me these great dressy black pants and this really beautiful black lacy, silky, kind of sparkly shirt that's see-through so I'm wearing a tight black tank top underneath. I'm borrowing my mom's black suede high-heeled boots that she used to wear with miniskirts in the sixties. I put on mascara and eyeliner and blush and I moussed my hair so it's red and I blew it dry so it's straight and not frizzy and it's bouncy and as cute as fucking hell. I just went out to the living room, steeling myself for my parents' negative response, but they looked at me and my mom said I looked "awesome." And I think she meant it. (Although I'd appreciate never hearing her use the word "awesome" again.) My dad said I looked beautiful and that even though he loved my natural hair color, he thought that the red was "totally funky." (Another couple words I'd appreciate never hearing come out of either of my parents' mouths again.) I do look "awesome" and "totally funky," however, so they're not wrong.

They then sat me down and said that they wanted to talk about the party I was having tonight. I thought, *Uh-oh. Here it comes. All the rules, the admonitions, the torrential rain on my parade . . .* But—drumroll please—they told me that as a special graduation present they're taking Hope to a hotel with them after graduation is over and my friends and I can have the place to ourselves tonight and that they'll be back at eleven tomorrow morning. What??!!?? How fucking cool is that? Pretty fucking cool. Gotta go. Next time I write anything, I'll be the proud bearer of an authentic high school diploma.

PARENTAL COMPENSATION (Brief Description)	LEVEL OF APPRECIATION 1-10 scale: 1 being Moderately Grateful, 10 being You Won't Hear Contempt in My Voice for a Week and I'll Clean My Room Without Being Asked
~~Getting me a puppy for my birthday~~	-10
Not getting on my case about fucking up the SATs and actually being uncharacteristically understanding and reassuring about my having to take them again in the fall	7
Writing my personal essay for my college applications so I don't have to	6
Overlooking the fact that my platonic relationship with Gregg has turned into an extremely nonplatonic one, thus letting me sleep over with him and spend as much time as I want with him without questioning my every move	14

Letting me have a graduation party at our unrenovated undivided loft space	10
Letting me have a graduation party at their unrenovated undivided loft space and then telling me at the last minute that they (and my little sister) are going to a hotel room for the night so my friends and I can have uninterrupted fun for as long as we want	100

The graduation party was a blast. I only got about three hours of sleep. It's nine-thirty a.m. and Jessica and Victoria are asleep in my parents' room. They're the only ones who slept over, although going to bed at six a.m. doesn't really count as sleeping over. Most everyone else cleared out around four, and Jessica and Victoria and I made pancakes and then crashed in a sticky, stoned, ecstatic stupor.

It was an incredible night. Truly. I don't think I'll ever forget it. Everyone was on their best behavior. Nothing got trashed. No one got out of control. We were all just happy. So happy. We all danced a lot. That's the best part about this loft, the open space to dance. At one point a bunch of us were dancing on my platform like it was a stage. Correction: It *is* a stage and we were the show.

A lot of people had brought their yearbooks to get them signed by people whom they'd missed in school. I had only seen Alexandra briefly on the last day (just long enough for her to cozy up to me sweetly so she could get an invite to my super-hip graduation loft party), so I had her sign mine. She was acting really nice and friendly. I guess we'd put the whole *Wiccan* incident behind us. She really is a good friend. Actually, she's not really a *good* friend, but we've been friends for such a long time that we forgive each other our faults. Well, I forgive her hers. Which are numerous. Here's what she wrote in my yearbook:

> *My God, am I going to miss you. This is such a lame place to try to explain all my feelings for you. I know that we've had our "troubles" over the years, but somehow we manage to tune in to each other in episodes and were able to connect on a deeper level each time. Cheers to cowboy boots and rum & Cokes and going out every night while the Frenchies were here. What a year. I don't even have to say good luck 'cause we know we're both gonna knock 'em dead out there. Shit. This is so sad. I miss you, baby, and you're not even gone yet. I'll always be here for you.*
> *Love, Alex*

I read that and I thought, *Maybe she wasn't all that bad. And maybe we're more alike than I want to admit. And maybe I was projecting so much on her. And . . . Nah, she's a pain in the ass, but she can be a blast sometimes and so it's worth putting up with her bullshit.* She left pretty early on, actually.

I looked for her and she was gone. She didn't say good-bye. I guess she'll "always be there" for me, except for tonight. She brought her new boyfriend, and I guess they wanted to go have sex. She hooked up with him when she went to the Spring Fling at the college she's attending in the fall. And now this guy's doing some sort of internship in New York this summer. Fan-fucking-tastic. Alexandra already has a boyfriend at college. And she's not even in college yet. I'll never know how she does it. But she does manage to do it. Over and over and over again.

Gregg was here for a while, but bowed out on the early side. I wanted him to stay (not wanting to miss out on a parentally unsupervised opportunity to cuddle up naked with him), but he said that he wanted me to hang out with my senior friends and have a chance to say good-bye without being distracted. I asked if he was really okay with that. He said he was and that he was going to get stoned and go to a special midnight showing of *All That Jazz*. It sounded like so much fun I almost wanted to go with him. He gave me a sweet, sexy kiss, put a freshly rolled pink joint into my hand, and left. What a man!

Jenny came to the party—wearing my sweater!! But she took it off at one point and then left without it. Either 'cause she was drunk or it was her way of giving it back. Doesn't matter. One good dry cleaning (man, that girl wears a lot of perfume) and my sweater and I will be one again (assuming that the dry-cleaning also shrinks it back down to fit my bustline). Just in time for summer.

Tommy B. was here and so was Danny B. and Mark L. And Sherry. She's not talking with an English accent anymore. She seemed really awkward coming in, but, honestly, I really didn't care. I was feeling so *magnanimous* with my classmates that they should all have been taking advantage of it while it lasted.

At the end of the party a bunch of us were standing around in a giant circle swaying and singing Steve Winwood's "Back in the High Life Again." Someone picked up a candle and then we all had candles in our hands while we swayed and sang. It was awesome. Corny, sure, but awesome. I was filled with forgiveness and love for my classmates and I felt truly forgiven and loved in return.

Eventually, everyone left except me (duh), Jessica and Victoria. We lit Gregg's hot pink joint, put on Patti Smith's version of "Because the Night" (which has been Victoria's and my anthem since we were in junior high), and danced around and sang loudly and off-key, and I realized that I was experiencing one of those rare, perfect, all-too-brief moments—when being a teenager doesn't suck.

teen·ag·er

(n.) a boy or girl between the ages of thirteen and nineteen

Anita Liberty takes the liberty of redefining the word "teenager" as a period of time in your life that sucks, except when it doesn't.

PARENTAL COMPENSATION (Grand Total)	PARENTAL REWARD (Grand Total)
87	127

(Huh. Who'd have guessed that my parents would end up coming out ahead? Good thing they let me have that party in their loft, or else they would have come out way behind. However, life is long and I'm sure they'll find many more opportunities to screw things up for me. In other words, the people at the nursing home shouldn't give away my parents' room yet. In fact, I should check to see if they're gonna need a deposit.)

THE

EPILOGUE
by Anita Liberty
(Again, the full-grown, very mature, non-teenage, adult one)

In general I'm not a fan of the epilogue. It just seems like some lame-ass way for an author to tie up loose ends and fill in some blanks she wasn't skilled enough to incorporate into the through-line of the book itself. But (and here comes my defense of this epilogue) since I put this book together with existing material and I now have the benefit of hindsight and of knowing how some of the situations I described actually resolved themselves, why wouldn't I provide you with that resolution? Hence, this epilogue is justified. Voilà.

First of all I never got taller than five feet two inches. And it's not so bad anymore. I'm still shorter than all my friends, but now I can call it "petite" and I don't feel like quite such a midget. Except there was a time in college when my friends decided that it might be entertaining to see how small a space I could fit into. Also, one time when a bunch of us were in Cape Cod for a summer weekend, I came upon a couple of my friends holding up my bathing suit and saying, "It's like for a six-year-old." And so the humiliation continued into my college years.

I ran into Adam years after I graduated from college and was able to tell him how he broke my heart in high school. I think he barely recognized me. We ran into each other on the subway and he was sort of just as cute and sexy as he had been in high school. Bastard. I was single at the time, so within the first ten minutes I had created a whole scenario where we were going to start dating and fall in love and how I'd actually end up with the cool guy after all and it would be such a great story at our wedding, etc. He flirted with me, touched my leg, my arm, held my hand, played with my fingers. He kissed me on the lips when we said good-bye. We exchanged phone numbers. And when I went to call him that night (because I've never believed in the convention of waiting for the guy to call first), I heard his outgoing message: "Sarah and Adam aren't home right now, but leave us a message and we'll be sure to get back to you." *Sarah?* Man, some things never change. I found out from Victoria (still the purveyor of all high school intel) that he'd been with this woman for years and they were engaged. Nice. Whatever.

Never heard from or ran into Monty again after high school. He was okay. He was good practice. But I don't think, in retrospect, that I ever had any real feelings for him. Going out with him was sort of like trying on a jacket that I knew didn't look good on me, but I *wanted* it to look good on me and it was on sale and they had it in my size, so I bought it and wore it around for a while, but never took the tags off and then, ultimately, decided to return it. Monty did have a beautiful body, though. I know that now, having seen lots and lots and lots of naked men. However, I'm still glad I didn't sleep with him.

I loved Gregg. I really did. He was my first true love. We had a great time together. And I'm glad that I had the experience of losing my virginity to someone I cared about who cared about me. Sorry to sound so sappy, but it made the experience that much more special. However, I ended up dumping him the minute my feet hit my college campus. I left for college convinced that we were going to stay together and transcend the physical distance and the vast disparity in our two separate existences—his still in high school and mine now in college—but the change of my heart was almost instantaneous. College was incredible. It was like Willy Wonka's chocolate factory with cute, sexy guys instead of gumdrops growing from the trees. I had my own room. There were no parents around. I could stay out late, drink beer, flirt with guys, get stoned, have sex. It was fantastic. I don't even remember really feeling bad for Gregg. And I learned later that he was hurt that I dumped him. Very hurt. However, when I ran into him on the street years and years later, he also had the pleasure of informing me that he was deeply in love and in a committed relationship . . . with a guy named Brad. So there ya go. I guess the fact that he loved Broadway musicals, pink strawberry-flavored rolling papers, and having lunch at lunchtime instead of sex with his *girlfriend* should have tipped me off. In his (our) defense, he told me that he hadn't quite figured out the parameters of his sexuality in high school, and he maintained that he loved me and loved being with me. No wonder he was such a great boyfriend—he was gay. I know how to pick 'em.

Which brings me to Alexandra's "hex." I'm convinced that, in fact, it was real and that it just lay dormant for twelve years, and maybe she was such an effective little Wiccan that she actually planned it that way—sort of like a time-release spell. Here's why I turned into a believer: At the end of my twenties I was going out with this guy Mitchell. We moved in together three and a half years into our relationship, and then he spontaneously dumped me for a woman named Heather (see my book, *How to Heal the Hurt by Hating*, for that whole story). I spent a lot of time and energy trying to dissect Mitchell's actions and trying to make sense of the end of that relationship. But when I started compiling this book and was reminded of Alexandra's hex, it all of a sudden made sense that Mitchell's dumping me had been the result of a twelve-year-old hex put on me by a high school witch. The moral of that story is that you should never cross a teenage Wiccan. Even if it seems like a lot of fun at the time.

My parents ended up renovating that rodent-infested undivided raw loft space in Manhattan. And now it is cool and beautiful and sexy. It was a great place to bring friends from college. It never ceases to impress people when they see it. And as a real estate investment, they couldn't have done better. It still doesn't make up for putting me on public display during my formative teenage years. Although, who knows how much spending time on my bedroom-stage influenced the fact that I ended up being a writer who performs her own work. So even though it was miserable at the time, I guess I should be grateful to my parents now. Hate that.

I'm sorry to have to report that the Future Fairy doesn't exist. At least, she never came to visit *me*. However, if she had, she would have told me that, in fact, it does all work out okay. My life is good. I have a gorgeous and brilliant and completely heterosexual husband and a spectacular daughter, who, even though she's many years away from being a teenager, is already able to speak to me at times with a tone dripping contempt. And so the circle of life is complete.

As for you, go have fun being a teenager. Or not. I don't care. It's your universe. The rest of us just live in it.

ACKNOWLEDGMENTS

Hey, Jennifer Klonsky, you're, like, the most awesome editor. I'm so glad we found each other this year. Doing this book just wouldn't have been the same without you. You're my new BFF! And now you have it in writing.

Jessica Sonkin, you're the grooviest design chick I've ever met. Your design of the cover and the inside of this book is just so freakin' amazing. You totally get it. And me. Thank you.

Yo, Bethany Buck and everyone at Simon Pulse (or, at least, everyone who's gonna work to make this book a success), thanks for giving me the support I need. I feel the love.

Oh, Daniel Greenberg, you are such a super-cool agent-guy. I'm lucky to know you and have you in my corner.

Cindy Ambers, my friend, my partner, my manager. What can I say? You and I have been together through it all. And I plan on us being together through whatever else comes our way. Major amounts of love.

My friend, Mark Tavani, I hang on your every word. Maybe because you read mine so carefully. I thank you from the bottom of my (bitter) heart.

Neeltje Henneman, Elizabeth Hannan, Allison Capone, Mary Duette & Jenne Blair—you guys were the first people (except for the person I sleep with) who laid eyes on this manuscript. You gave me the encouragement I needed to keep going. (And I needed a lot!)

A special shout-out to my family for understanding how I alter details to make myself look better, how I change names to protect the guilty and how the truth is that I adore you, Mom and JTW, no matter how much I mock you in my work. And that I also adore my dad, even though he's no longer around. I miss him pretty much constantly. And I know he would have loved this book, even the mocking. The man could easily out-mock me and I consider myself a pretty skilled mocker. He taught me well.

And, finally, even though they already got a mention in the epilogue, I'd like to acknowledge my adorable husband (on whom I still have a crush) and my winsome wee daughter (who recently told me that she'll never be mad at me, not even when she's a teenager . . . I told her not to make promises she couldn't keep). You guys make me feel like the center of the universe, in the best way possible.

ANITA LIBERTY

is the author of this book. Oh, and of two other books. And she's written a bunch of other stuff, like one-person shows and television pilots and webisodes and screenplays. And she lives in New York. And she's married. And she has a kid. And she's only seventeen! (At least, she is on the inside. Where it counts.)